T0316224

Bello:

hidden talent rediscovered!

Bello is a digital only imprint of Pan Macmillan,
established to breathe new life into previously published,
classic books.

At Bello we believe in the timeless power of the imagination,
of good story, narrative and entertainment and we want to use
digital technology to ensure that many more readers
can enjoy these books into the future.

We publish in ebook and Print on Demand formats
to bring these wonderful books to new audiences.

About Bello:

www.panmacmillan.com/imprints/bello

About the author:

www.panmacmillan.com/author/paulsomers

B E L L

Paul Somers

Paul Somers is the pen name of Paul Winterton (1908–2001). He was born in Leicester and educated at the Hulme Grammar School, Manchester and Purley County School, Surrey, after which he took a degree in Economics at London University. He was on the staff of *The Economist* for four years, and then worked for fourteen years for the *London News Chronicle* as reporter, leader writer and foreign correspondent. He was assigned to Moscow from 1942–5, where he was also the correspondent of the BBC's Overseas Service.

After the war he turned to full-time writing of detective and adventure novels and produced more than forty-five books. His work was serialized, televised, broadcast, filmed and translated into some twenty languages. He is noted for his varied and unusual backgrounds – which have included Russia, newspaper offices, the West Indies, ocean sailing, the Australian outback, politics, mountaineering and forestry – and for never repeating a plot.

Paul Somers was a founder member and first joint secretary of the Crime Writers' Association.

Paul Somers

BEGINNER'S LUCK

First published in 1958 by Collins

This edition published 2012 by Bello
an imprint of Pan Macmillan, a division of Macmillan Publishers Limited
Pan Macmillan, 20 New Wharf Road, London N1 9RR
Basingstoke and Oxford
Associated companies throughout the world

www.panmacmillan.com/imprints/bello
www.curtisbrown.co.uk

ISBN 978-1-4472-1593-6 EPUB
ISBN 978-1-4472-1592-9 POD

Copyright © Paul Somers, 1958

The right of Paul Somers to be identified as the
author of this work has been asserted in accordance
with the Copyright, Designs and Patents Act 1988.

Every effort has been made to contact the copyright holders of the material
reproduced in this book. If any have been inadvertently overlooked, the publisher
will be pleased to make restitution at the earliest opportunity.

You may not copy, store, distribute, transmit, reproduce or otherwise
make available this publication (or any part of it) in any form, or by any means
(electronic, digital, optical, mechanical, photocopying, recording or otherwise),
without the prior written permission of the publisher. Any person who does
any unauthorized act in relation to this publication may be liable to
criminal prosecution and civil claims for damages.

The Macmillan Group has no responsibility for the information provided by
any author websites whose address you obtain from this book ('author websites').
The inclusion of author website addresses in this book does not constitute
an endorsement by or association with us of such sites or the content,
products, advertising or other materials presented on such sites.

This book remains true to the original in every way. Some aspects may appear
out-of-date to modern-day readers. Bello makes no apology for this, as to retrospectively
change any content would be anachronistic and undermine the authenticity of the original.
Bello has no responsibility for the content of the material in this book. The opinions
expressed are those of the author and do not constitute an endorsement by,
or association with, us of the characterization and content.

A CIP catalogue record for this book is available from the British Library.

Visit **www.panmacmillan.com** to read more about all our books
and to buy them. You will also find features, author interviews and
news of any author events, and you can sign up for e-newsletters
so that you're always first to hear about our new releases.

Chapter One

The day I started work as a reporter on the London *Daily Record* was my first day as a newspaperman anywhere, and I felt pretty scared as well as excited when, just before eleven o'clock, I presented myself at the office in Fleet Street. But I needn't have worried. Blair, the News Editor, couldn't have been more friendly and considerate. He introduced me to one or two other members of the staff who were around and then, shortly before twelve, he put me in the charge of an elderly reporter named Furnival, a man with a slow drawl and charming Edwardian manners, who would "show me the ropes." We were to go out to Hampshire together and do a story about the drought, which was supposed to be bad there. The first thing that happened was that Furnival drew ten pounds from the cashier. "The essential preliminary to any story," he said, as we crossed the road to El Vino's for a glass of sherry. We had two glasses, and then he said there was no point in breaking our necks so we might as well have lunch at the Cheshire Cheese before we started. We had steak pie and some excellent claret, and Furnival talked of the days when Fleet Street still had dignity and reporters came to work in top hats and frock coats and leader writers wrote their columns with a bottle of port at the elbow. After we'd banqueted, he suggested we should collect his car and so avoid the discomfort of public transport. We took a cab to his delightful home in Putney, where he introduced me to his wife and showed me round his walled garden. About three, he got out an ancient car, and we set off at a leisurely pace for deepest Hampshire. We stopped for tea at an old-world inn around five, and there was still no sign of any story. Afterwards we went along to the village that Blair had mentioned and called on a smallholder and a couple of cottagers and Furnival asked if there was a drought and they said there was a bit of a water shortage and Furnival listened with attentive sympathy for a few moments and then said we'd have to be getting back. He dropped me off at an Underground station, and said I needn't bother to do anything about the story as he'd phone it from home. Next morning there was a bright quarter of a column in the *Record* about the Hampshire drought. I couldn't think where he'd got it all from, and decided that I couldn't have been listening properly. Anyhow, it had been a most pleasant outing.

On the second day I was given my first solo assignment—a Ladies' Archery Tournament in Kent. Blair said, "I expect you'll want some money," and wrote out a chit for five pounds, which I cashed on my way out. I supposed there'd be a day of reckoning some time, but no one had mentioned that yet. I drove down in my Riley and lunched on the way and arrived at the field in good time for the start. The competitors were picturesquely costumed and there was a lot of green sward and dappled shade and everything looked most attractive. The secretary of the club welcomed me with enthusiasm—I seemed to be the only reporter from a national paper—and readily gave me all the information I wanted. I watched the tournament from a comfortable deck-chair in the company of a pretty girl who was dressed like Maid Marian and who talked knowledgeably of "golds" and "perfect ends" and "Hereford Rounds" and got me the names of the winning team when it was all over. We had a slap-up tea in a marquee, and afterwards I retired to the car and composed a careful descriptive piece and phoned it. When I opened the *Record* next morning I found it hadn't been used—but I wasn't too depressed. I'd made a start, and I felt I was going to like reporting very much indeed.

On the third day I was on the four o'clock turn, and for the first time I met the Night News Editor, a man named Hatcher. He was thin, grizzled and fiftyish, and he had an abrupt, parade-ground manner that took me straight back to Catterick. He barked "Who the devil are you?" when I went in to report to him, and snorted when I told him, and said if he wanted me he'd let me know. For the next four hours I sat on my bottom doing nothing. I was just beginning to feel very hungry when Hatcher rushed out of the News Room in a state of bloodshot excitement yelling, "Curtis!—fire!—Whitechapel High Street!" I got a taxi to Whitechapel High Street. There was a light drizzle falling. As far as I could make out, the fire was in an upper floor of a block of shops. There were a lot of fire engines and police cars and ambulances outside, and hundreds of people standing around watching. The smoke was thick in the street and the traffic congestion was pretty bad. I waved my Press pass at a policeman and tried to get nearer the scene but he told me to stand back. He seemed very harassed. I tackled a sergeant, but he wouldn't let me through, either. I didn't seem to be very successful with policemen. I tried to sneak through the cordon unnoticed but the sergeant spotted me and threatened me with arrest for obstruction. From where I was I couldn't see a thing because of the smoke. I started to question some of the bystanders, and presently I found a man in a house opposite who was able to help me. He said the fire was in a furrier's shop and the furrier had been taken to hospital with bad burns. I got the name of the furrier from him, and felt very cheered. I wrote out the story under a lamp, and phoned it, and went back to the office. Hatcher greeted me with "You're a bloody fine reporter!" and thrust a bit of agency copy at me. The agency said that the fire had been at a pawnbroker's and that three small children had been rescued by fire-escape. "Couldn't even get the bloody place right!" Hatcher said disgustedly. "Why don't you check your facts? Do you realise if your story had gone into the paper, that furrier would have been after us for damages?" He tore my copy into small pieces, threw the bits on the floor, and barked "Good night!"

That was the third day.

Chapter Two

I was in a pretty dejected frame of mind when I got to the office next morning. I positively slunk into the Reporters' Room. I glanced at the correspondence rack, where official communications were always put, half expecting to find a memo from Blair giving me a week's notice. With relief, I saw that my pigeon hole was empty. However, my blunder of the previous night hadn't passed entirely without comment. It was the custom among the *Record's* reporters to use the woodwork around the pigeon holes for making topical cracks about each other, usually scurrilous. The technique was to snip suitable words from newspaper headlines and cunningly paste them together. Until now, the space around my pigeon hole had been bare. Now it wasn't. Someone had pasted up, MAN SUED BY ANGRY FURRIER. The night staff had obviously been enjoying itself.

I reported to Blair, who glanced up from a sea of papers, grunted, and returned immediately to his work. I went back into the Reporters' Room. It was a large, airy room, separated from the News Room by a glass partition. There were fifteen or twenty desks, each with a typewriter and a few drawers; half a dozen piles of telephone directories and reference books; some desk telephones; and a lot of waste baskets. At the end of the room, where the shorthand writers sat, there was a battery of telephone booths. So far, the only occupant of the room was a man named Martin, who was going through the morning papers with a blue pencil marking stories that might be worth following up. He was a quiet, studious-looking man with thick horn-rimmed glasses, who seemed to spend part of his time as a reporter and part as Deputy Assistant

News Editor. He had two distinct personalities, according to which job he was doing. To-day, the reporter seemed uppermost. He gave me a friendly smile.

"I hear you had your baptism of fire last night."

"I fell flat on my face," I said ruefully.

"Well, it's a position we've all been in."

"Really?"

"Of course. Very upsetting, but good for the soul! I shouldn't worry—there's always a to-morrow in this job."

I felt grateful.

After a few moments two more reporters came in, both of whom I'd met before—a woman named Mabel Learoyd, grey, spinsterish, very much the "old hand," and Jack Lawson, one of the crime specialists, a slim, pallid man of thirty or so with a rather knowing air. He was followed almost at once by another man, a stranger to me, who turned out to be the Chief Reporter, Fred Hunt. He'd been away all the week on an out-of-town story.

Martin said, "Fred, meet the new boy—Hugh Curtis."

Hunt gave me a shrewd look, and nodded. He was a dark, handsome, immaculately-dressed man, exuding vitality and confidence. He took some brushes from a drawer and began to polish his shoes, though they were already mirror-bright. "I heard about you," he said, and paused. "You wouldn't be any relation of Sir Jocelyn Curtis, would you?"

"I'm his son," I said, in as neutral a tone as I could manage.

"Friend of the Chairman, isn't he?"

"Yes, he is."

Hunt regarded me for a moment in gloomy silence. Then he turned to Lawson and said, "Seen any good fires lately, Jack?"

"I hear there was a big one in Whitechapel last night," Lawson said. "At a furrier's, I'm told."

I smiled rather sheepishly.

Martin said, "It's your turn to buy the coffee, Fred."

"What, when I've been away all week? Not on your life! Curtis can buy it—he's probably rolling, anyway."

"I'll be glad to," I said. I dialled the canteen and ordered five coffees. Mabel Learoyd asked for hers black, with a vanilla ice and a packet of charcoal biscuits. "I've a touch of indigestion," she explained.

There was a short lull in the talk. Presently the News Room door opened with a bang, and a perky youth came out, whistling softly between his teeth, and gave Hunt a cutting. "Mr. Blair thought you might like to see this," he said.

Hunt took the cutting between his finger and thumb as though it were contaminated and dropped it into the waste basket with scarcely a glance. "Now why would he think that ...? Ah, here's the coffee! Morning, Phyllis! Have a good time last night, Phyllis?"

The waitress said, "None of your lip!" and passed the cups around.

Lawson looked up from a copy of the *Courier* he was reading. The *Courier* was the *Record's* chief rival. "I say, Fred—do you see Mollie Bourne's got herself mixed up in a story again? That girl doesn't report the news, she makes it!"

"What's she been up to this time?"

"Dined with Alonzo just before he caught that plane last night. ... Drove him to the airport! What a woman!" Lawson picked up his coffee cup and gave me a nod of acknowledgment as he drank. "I suppose you haven't run into Mollie Bourne yet, Curtis, have you?"

"No," I said, "who is she?"

"Reporter on the *Courier*. Always getting into trouble. Always getting scoops. If you want to do well in Fleet Street, old boy, here's a tip—keep your eye on Mollie! That's right, Fred, isn't it?"

"That's right," said Hunt. "Golden rule."

"What's she like?" I asked.

Lawson leered. "Very enjoyable, I should think. Smashing redhead."

"She's a damned good reporter," Martin said, in his deputy-assistant-news-editorial voice.

The News Room door banged again. This time the perky youth made a bee-line for me. "Mr. Blair says you're to get a bright story out of this," he announced, and slapped a journal down in front of me. It was the *Economist*.

I looked round at the others. They were all grinning like apes.

"I can't read that sexy stuff," Lawson said. "Excites me too much . . .! Ah, here's old Smee—late as usual. Afternoon, Smee!"

Smee was a big, shambling man, with a perpetually hurt look as though he'd been cruelly baited. I'd met him already. I ordered another coffee.

Martin, blue-pencilling steadily, said, "You're looking a bit under the weather, George."

Smee said, "That bastard Hatcher kept me out till three o'clock this morning. I'll do that bastard one of these days. He'll go too far, you'll see."

"He's all right," Hunt said. "You've just got to know how to handle him."

"It's all very well for you," said Smee. "You're never on the late turn."

"I used to be. The only trouble with Hatcher is that his nerves are shot to pieces. What he needs is a good bad woman."

"Don't we all?" said Lawson.

"Heart of gold, really," Hunt said.

"When I tear it out," Smee said darkly, "we'll see!" He took a sheaf of papers from his drawer and six bottles of different coloured inks and started to work on what was reputed to be a very profitable racing system.

It was a quarter to twelve now, and judging by the activity in the News Room Blair's preparations for the morning conference, which always took place at noon, were reaching a climax. Presently he came bustling out himself. He was a short, square man, with enormously powerful shoulders, and he bore down on us like a rather fussy bulldozer. I turned a page of the *Economist* and tried to seem interested in the "Active Securities." Blair proposed an assignment to Hunt that Hunt didn't like. Hunt addressed him as "Blair" and talked back like an equal. There was a short, testy argument. Blair had a way of saying "M'm?" every few seconds when anyone argued with him, which gave the quite erroneous impression that he was being slowly won over. In the end, of course, he had his way, and Hunt departed, grumbling. Mabel Learoyd was dispatched to a luncheon, with her charcoal biscuits in her handbag, and Smee was sent to meet a V.I.P. off a train. I was ignored. Martin went to help out at the News Desk while Blair attended conference. Lawson opened a paper-backed thriller and put his feet up. "Quiet day for crime," he said, winking.

I was to remember that—later!

The conference lasted half an hour, and then the News Room came to life again. I looked through the glass partition and saw that Blair was grinning hugely. He was usually in a better temper, Lawson said, when conference was over. After a moment he came quietly out, and approached me as though he were going to impart some tremendous secret. "Oh, Curtis," he said, "here's a story for you. A cannon ball's disappeared from Lodden Castle in Sussex. You might get down there and find out what's happened to it."

The symbolism wasn't lost on me. In fact, I thought at first that he was simply pulling my leg. But when he'd gone, Lawson said, "Well, good-bye, Curtis. Into the valley of death!"

"You don't mean he was serious?" I said.

"Sure he was serious."

"But it's such a trivial thing. What's the point?"

"Yours not to reason why, old boy. Probably your penance! Anyway, why should you worry?—it's a day out of town on expenses."

I closed my desk, and went and collected my hat from the stand. As I passed the correspondence rack I saw that a new headline had been pasted beside my name. This time it read: BARONET'S SON ON ARSON CHARGE.

Chapter Three

I was still smarting a little over my unpromising assignment as I headed the Riley for Sussex. Not that I blamed Blair, or any of them, for having a bit of fun at my expense. I'd certainly asked for it, right from the beginning. I'd gone into Fleet Street by the wrong door, the door of influence, instead of the hard, slow way via police court reporting and a local paper. I'd done it with my eyes open, accepting the risks, because after three years at Oxford and two more in the army I'd felt there simply wasn't time to start at the bottom. I'd intended to work hard and make up for it that way; to learn quickly, and do well. Instead, I'd made a botch of things. Naturally, the professionals were gloating. All I wished was that they'd taken it out of me by sending me on another fire, in which case I doubted if any police cordon would have stopped me. This cannon ball story was not merely humiliating—it held out no hope of redemption.

However, my spirits slowly improved. Memories, I'd been told, were short in Fleet Street, and meanwhile it was a heavenly day, warm and sunny. There were certainly worse ways of spending a May afternoon than cruising through a pleasant countryside. I drove at an unhurried pace, enjoying the scenery, and it was nearly four o'clock when I reached Lodden. It proved to be a most attractive little hamlet, set well back from a busy main road. It had a picturesque parish church, one shop, an inviting-looking pub called the Castle Arms, and a few old cottages, all clustered round an ancient stone bridge across the River Lod. The castle, of which only the top of a tower was visible from the village, stood on rising ground about half a mile from the church. I drove as near to it as

I could get, parking the Riley in the castle car park beside a wooden tea-room that, rather surprisingly, was shuttered. The approach to the castle was through an iron kissing-gate and up a field path. I'd taken it for granted that I should get all the information I wanted at the castle itself, but when I reached the gate I found a notice there which said: LODDEN CASTLE. CLOSED FOR REPAIRS. REOPENING JUNE 1ST.

That shook me a little. I'd assumed that if a cannon ball really had disappeared, it had probably been taken by some sky-larking youngsters during a visit. Now that seemed less likely.

A piece of paper tacked to the notice board gave the name and address of the caretaker as T. Figgis, Rose Cottage, Lodden, and I strolled back to the village to look him up. I soon found the cottage, a charming blend of thatch and old timber—but not, unfortunately, T. Figgis. His wife, a fair-haired girl who was herself preparing to leave the house as I arrived, said that her husband had gone off to London that afternoon "on a course," and that she expected him to be away for nearly a week. When the castle reopened in seven days' time, she explained, he was to be the official guide as well as the caretaker, and he was now being briefed for the job. I asked her if it was true that a cannon ball was missing and she said it was and that it had been taken two days ago and that they had no idea who might have taken it. I asked her if anyone had been allowed inside the castle while it had been officially closed and she said No, only the workmen, and they'd finished a week ago, and she was sorry she couldn't stop and talk now but she had a bus to catch. I felt, and possibly looked, a bit worried about where I was going to get hold of enough information to make a story, and she said kindly that perhaps I'd like to look over the castle myself now I was here and if so she thought it would be all right as I was from a newspaper. Looking over the castle seemed a poor substitute for a talk with T. Figgis, but it was certainly better than nothing, so I thanked her and she gave me the key, a massive object that made me feel like a beefeater, together with a short "Guide to Lodden Castle" for which I paid her ninepence. I promised to leave the key under a box beside the back door when

I'd finished with it, and was just thinking up another question or two to fire at her when the bus arrived and carried her off.

I walked slowly back to the kissing-gate, glancing through the introduction to the guide book as I went. There was a whimsical paragraph about some medieval legend, which I didn't pay much attention to, and a few historical facts, which I marked for possible use later. The castle had been built, it seemed, in the late fourteenth century to command the waterway of the river Lod at a time when naval raids by the French were feared—though in fact they'd never materialised. It had suffered a short siege during the Wars of the Roses and had played a small part in the Civil War. It had been privately owned until 1939 and had then been presented to a Trust. That was about all. By this time I had reached the gate, and I set off up the field path to see what the castle looked like.

It was in a wonderfully fine state of preservation. It was built on a simple rectangle—about fifty yards long by forty wide, the book said—and its crenellated walls, seven feet thick and forty feet high, were all intact. Except for a few narrow loopholes, the walls were blank. At each corner there was a round tower, and in the centre of each flank a square tower, and the towers, I read, were sixty feet high. The whole pile rose majestically from a broad moat, carpeted with water lilies and fringed with hazel bushes. Ancient oaks and elms provided a splendid background. Apart from a small wooden hut near the entrance, which was obviously used for the sale of tickets when the castle was open to the public, there wasn't a building in sight. The place had a wonderful air of serenity and peace, and I could imagine that T. Figgis quite enjoyed his custodianship.

An earthen causeway led across the moat to a pointed gate arch, with a spiked portcullis that seemed to hang threateningly but was in fact well rusted into its socket. I thrust my key into the big mortice lock and wrestled with it for a moment or two and finally succeeded in swinging one of the halves of the huge oak door back on its creaking hinges. Inside, there was a broad passage with some fine groined vaulting, curiously pierced by a number of large circular holes. I referred to the book, and discovered that they were "*meurtrières*" or "murder holes," through which the old-time defenders had poured their molten lead and pitch as the enemy stormed in. Beyond, there was a rectangular courtyard, grassed over with well-kept turf, and surrounded by remnants of partition walls. Ferns and wallflowers grew in profusion from the sheltered crannies of the grey-green, lichened stone, and the air was deliciously scented. It was a most satisfying place, tranquil as an abbey cloister.

So far I had seen no sign of any cannon or cannon balls, either outside or inside the castle, but now as I glanced around the courtyard I spotted what was undoubtedly some sort of gun, and I walked quickly across to it. There was a guard chain around it, and a descriptive panel was planted in the grass beside it. The gun, I read, was a replica of a fifteenth-century siege gun, or bombard, the original of which had been dredged up out of the moat and given to a museum. The stone shot lying beside the gun, the panel said, was also a replica. It had a diameter of 15 inches and weighed 150 lbs. There was a depression in the grass where the shot had lain, but the shot was no longer there. This, I had to conclude, was the missing "cannon ball."

By now, I was beginning to feel distinctly intrigued. The physical effort involved in moving a stone shot weighing nearly a hundredweight and a half must have been very considerable. If it had been taken away altogether, it had presumably been manhandled all the way to the kissing-gate, a tremendous undertaking. And why should anyone want to steal a stone shot, particularly one that was only a replica? It was possible, of course, that it hadn't been stolen—some vandal might simply have rolled it into the moat for a joke or a bet. But what opportunity had there been for anyone to do that, when the castle was closed to visitors? Certainly no one could have broken into such a place. I wished more than ever that I could have had a word with T. Figgis.

I went on to explore the rest of the castle, and it didn't take me long. Though the outer walls were so well preserved, they were in fact no more than a beautiful shell. The guide book indicated the sites of places like the Lord's Kitchen, the Buttery and Pantry, the Retainers' Hall, the Bower and the Chapel, but they had either been deliberately demolished in some earlier age or had fallen into total ruin. I inspected the remains of several tile-backed fireplaces, and a shallow hole near the entrance gate that had once been a dungeon, and a well in the basement of one of the towers that was supposed to have supplied water to the kitchens. The towers themselves, with one exception, were all hollow and stairless. The exception was a square one directly opposite the main entrance and commanding what had evidently been a second entrance to the castle, now walled up. I went through a wooden door and climbed a spiral stone staircase dimly lit by loopholes. Half-way up the staircase there was access to a first floor chamber, bare and cold, and at the top of the flight there was another, heavier door, opening on to a flat concrete roof some twenty feet square. It was here, apparently, that much of the repair work had been done, for I could see several places where holes and cracks in the stone had been filled and strengthened with new cement. A waist-high parapet, carried on heavy stone corbels, overhung the sides of the tower, leaving a gap a foot wide between the parapet and the walls down which more nasty liquids had doubtless been poured on the heads of scaling parties. The gap was protected now by three narrow iron slats, an inch or two apart, so that one could still look down the sides of the walls to the moat and yet tread with safety.

Except to the east, where the ground rose gently to high woods, the view from the roof was extensive. Far to the north I made out a faint line of smooth blue hills, the last outcrop of the South Downs. To the west and south, rich, level pastures stretched away to the horizon. The countryside looked empty and unspoilt. At the foot of the castle slope, the river Lod wound its way quietly through the water meadows.

I stayed up there for a few minutes, admiring the scene and enjoying the sense of remoteness that one had at the top of the tower. Then I finished my circuit of the castle, locked the door behind me, and took the key back to Rose Cottage. I had had a pleasant little excursion, but I hadn't got very much further with the story. So far, it seemed to be nothing but question marks. I talked about the missing stone to one or two villagers, but they didn't appear to be taking the loss very seriously and none of them looked at all deprived. I sought out the village policeman, P.C. Mathers, and asked him if the loss had been officially reported and he said that Tom Figgis had mentioned it to him and he'd mentioned it to his superior, but as the shot was of no great value and they were short-handed anyway, nothing had been done about it. He agreed it was a "funny business" but he hadn't any theories to offer. And that seemed to be that.

I wrote my story in the lounge of the Castle Arms, padding out the few facts with a bit of description and some stuff from the guide book, and at six o'clock I got on the phone to the office and dictated it to a shorthand writer. Afterwards I was put through to the News Desk, the unbreakable routine, and Hatcher was there, and I started to tell him what I'd been doing.

He cut me short. "Have you found the cannon ball?" he snarled.

"Well, no . . ." I began. "The fact is . . ."

"Then stay there till you've bloody well found it," he said, and hung up.

I made a mental note to ask Smee to cut me in on any heart-tearing-out party he happened to be organising in the near future. Meanwhile, I'd obviously got to grin and bear it. It hadn't occurred to me that I might be kept out of town overnight on such a paltry story, but luckily I'd taken a bit of advice that Furnival had given me and I had a small bag already packed in the car against just this sort of emergency. I booked a room at the Castle Arms, which I'd already discovered to be a homely, do-as-you-please sort of inn with a tradition of comfort. Then I rang the News Desk again to let them know where I was staying, and went off to find the bar and drown my sorrows. There was only one other customer there, a girl. She was sitting on a high stool with her back to the door, sipping tomato juice and doing a crossword puzzle in the *Courier*. The back view was distinctly promising—she had a mass of rich chestnut hair, a glorious colour, perfectly set off by a cool summer frock with unusual shades of green in it. I ordered a small bitter, and as she turned to see who had come in, the promise was more than fulfilled. She had dark eyes and a creamy complexion and a beautifully shaped mouth. She was lovely.

I felt sure it couldn't be a coincidence. I said, "Excuse me—but are you by any chance Mollie Bourne?"

She gave me a haughty stare. After a moment she said, "I am—yes. Who are you?"

"My name's Hugh Curtis. I'm a reporter on the *Records*."

She thawed at once. "Are you, though? In that case, draw up a stool."

I drew up a stool. Close to, she looked even more attractive. She was exquisitely groomed, immensely self-possessed. Yet she couldn't have been more than twenty-three or twenty-four.

"You're new, aren't you?" she said.

I nodded. "Straight from the Mint!"

"I suppose you're on this castle story, too?"

"Yes . . . I quite thought I had it to myself. Isn't it rather small stuff for a star reporter?"

She smiled. "I happen to like Lodden Castle—my people used to live not far away—and the story sounded mildly amusing so I suggested I should cover it."

"Now that's what I call a civilised way of running an office," I said. "I'm afraid I was sent here as a punishment. Same principle as running round the barrack square with a full pack."

"Why, what have you done?"

"Fallen down on a story." I told her about the fire, not without a certain relish. In retrospect, it was beginning to seem rather funny. She thought so, too.

"Well, you're not likely to fall down on this story," she said.

"I'm not so sure. I've been told to stay here until I find the stone!"

"That sounds like Hatcher!"

"It was, as a matter of fact."

"He's just a sadist. If you take my advice you'll relax and enjoy yourself."

"I'm beginning to," I said. I looked at her empty glass. "What about a real drink?"

"I'd sooner have another tomato juice, if you don't mind. I have to watch my figure."

I'd been watching it, too, and it wasn't any hardship. "Keeping an eye on Mollie," in Lawson's phrase, would be a pleasure.

I ordered the drinks. Then I said, "Did you send a long piece about the castle?"

"Good heavens, no. There wasn't much to say, was there?"

I agreed, with relief, that there wasn't. "All the same, it's quite interesting," I said. "What do *you* think happened to the stone?"

She gave a slight shrug. "Just a piece of hooliganism, I should think. It's probably at the bottom of the moat."

"Yes, but how did the chap get into the castle?"

She gave me a quizzical smile. "That's the mystery, isn't it?" she said.

"In any case, it would have been quite a job to get the stone even as far as the moat."

"But not impossible—not for a big man." She looked me up and down, appraisingly. "I should think you could carry 150 pounds, couldn't you?"

"To the moat? Just about—but it wouldn't be much fun."

"Whoever did it was probably crackers," she said. "You know—strength of madness!" She sounded a bit bored with the subject, so I didn't pursue it.

"How long do you think you'll be staying?" I asked her.

"Over to-morrow, anyway. I'm due for a few days off, and I thought of doing some sketching at the castle."

"Sketching? Are you good?"

"Not really. I dabble a bit, that's all . . ." She began to gather up her belongings.

"If you're going to be around," I said, "perhaps you'd join me for dinner to-night?"

"And help you to relax?"

"That's the idea."

"It seems quite a pleasant one." She finished her tomato juice and slid off her stool. She was tall for a girl, but not too tall. She was slim, but not in the least fragile-looking. In fact, I couldn't see a single flaw in her. "I'll see you in the dining-room at seven, then," she said.

I was waiting for her. She was fifteen minutes late. She'd changed into something stream-lined and looked very elegant. We had a cosy corner in the little dining-room and the steak was good and so was the bottle of Chateau Latour '37 that the manager had personally dug up for me from the cellar. Mollie was delightful company. From the way Lawson had described her, I'd expected her to be very hard-boiled in the Fleet Street sense, but there was no sign of that. Her conversation was bright, but not in the least tough. Naturally, we talked "shop" most of the time. I asked her how long she'd been on the *Courier* and she said two years. Apparently she'd gone there straight from Lady Margaret Hall and, like me, had never been near a local paper, which I found encouraging. She told me about some of the stories she'd been on, and one or two of her experiences struck me as pretty hair-raising. She seemed to find them merely amusing. She had tremendous zest, and obviously enjoyed every minute of her work.

After the second glass of wine I asked her, in a mock-interview manner, to what she attributed her spectacular success.

"If you must know," she said with a mischievous smile, "it's just a confidence trick. If a reasonably attractive girl is sent to cover a fashion show, nobody takes any special notice of her. If she turns up to report a murder, everyone falls over backwards to help her because they're sorry for her."

"In fact, you concentrate on the men and use everything you've got?"

"Almost everything," she said. "One has to keep a reserve for contingencies."

I asked her how it was that she managed to get mixed up personally in so many stories, and she thought it was just an excess of zeal. She told me how she'd been sent to cover a Record Walk across the Cumberland fells at Easter, and had tried to do the walk herself, and had had to be rescued from a mist-covered peak at night by an R.A.F. Mountain Rescue team. That started me off about the Lakes, where I'd done quite a bit of rock-climbing in the Long Vac. before my call-up, and she turned out to be as good a listener as she was a talker.

It was after eleven when we finally said good night—and that was still too early for me. I put the lights out in the lounge, because everyone else had gone to bed, and we crept quietly upstairs. Her room was number 6, two doors from mine. She lingered for a moment at her door, and the heady thought crossed my mind that she was going to ask me in for a nightcap—that she might even regard me as a contingency! But she just smiled very charmingly and said it had been a delightful evening and wished me "Good night." I went to my own room in a mental whirl, and it wasn't just the wine. At that moment I couldn't have cared less about Hatcher, or the office, or stone shots weighing a hundredweight and a half. I had met, I felt sure, the one woman in my life!

Chapter Four

There was no sign of Mollie when I went down to breakfast at nine next morning. I thought perhaps she was sleeping late, as it was her day off, but it turned out that she'd already breakfasted and gone out.

I'd asked the hotel to get me the *Courier* as well as the *Record*, and they were both beside my plate. I opened my own paper first and looked eagerly through it—but once again not a line of my story had been used. I was disappointed, but hardly surprised. What I'd sent hadn't amounted to much; and there was a sensational "missing frogman" story on page one that must have squeezed a lot of other things out. I picked up the *Courier*, feeling fairly sure that Mollie wouldn't have got much of a show, either. But I was wrong. On page three she had a signed story with the Lodden dateline and a picture of the castle and a caption across three columns. I read what she'd written with mounting dismay. It ran:

"Mystery broods to-day over the lovely castle of Lodden in Sussex.

"Ever since Sir Bedford de Courtenay leapt to his death from the battlements after an interrupted tryst with his mistress the Lady Blanche, the inhabitants of this charming Sussex village have believed the castle to be haunted. Strange noises have been heard at night, and there are villagers who refuse to go near the place after dark.

"But now the question is being asked, Can a ghost carry a stone shot weighing 150 pounds? For that is the object that was mysteriously removed from the inner courtyard two days ago.

"The castle, which has been closed for repairs since the autumn, was locked up at the time, and Mr. Tom Figgis, the caretaker, told me to-day that the key was in his possession when the theft occurred. The castle is moated, and the walls are 40 feet high, so that entry is virtually impossible except through the main gate.

"Mr. Figgis himself doesn't believe in weight-lifting ghosts, and he has his own theory. Four years ago, a key was taken from the lock of the main gate by some visitor. As the castle contains nothing of value, the lock was never changed. Are the two thefts connected?

"If so, the mystery deepens. For why should anyone return after four years to remove a hundredweight and a half of completely worthless stone?"

I put the paper down, feeling pretty sick. Obviously, I'd failed again. It was no use telling myself that I'd been unlucky—that if I'd arrived early enough to see Figgis, as Mollie had done, or if Mrs. Figgis hadn't been in such a hurry to catch her bus, I should probably have heard about the lost key, too. The fact was that I hadn't, and excuses wouldn't get me anywhere. Even if I had heard about it, I doubted if I'd have been able to compose such a gem of a story. It was a neat professional job, eye-catching, intriguing, comprehensive, and brief. I'd never felt more of a tiro than at that moment—not even after the fire. It was all very humbling.

I drank my coffee moodily. It was naïve of me, I knew, but I couldn't help feeling piqued with Mollie. No wonder she hadn't wanted to talk about the castle!—no wonder she'd said, "It's a mystery," when I'd asked how anyone could have got in! And all that disarming chatter over dinner! There she'd sat, phonily friendly, knowing all the time that she'd done me down and that I was going to look pretty silly in the morning. And I'd detected no toughness! If a light and unimportant story like this could bring out such duplicity in her, what, I wondered, would she be like over a big one? The imagination boggled.

Well, I'd had my lesson, and it was no good dwelling on it. I went out to the little shop and bought all the other papers that I could get and read through them with a conscientiousness that even Hatcher couldn't have criticised, just to make sure I wasn't missing anything. Afterwards I continued to hang around the hotel lobby, feeling pretty sure that the office would be on the blower before long to tear off a strip. And sure enough, just before eleven there was a call for me. It was Martin at the other end, doing the Deputy Assistant News Editor part of his Jekyll-and-Hyde act. His voice was quiet and restrained, as always, but it had an edge to it.

"Hallo, Curtis," he said. "Have you seen Mollie Bourne's story about the castle, by any chance?"

I said I had.

"Pity you didn't get it. All that guide book stuff you sent cuts no ice at all, you know. You're supposed to be a reporter, not a Baedeker. Blair's pretty annoyed."

I wiped the sweat from the earpiece of the receiver, and said I could imagine it and that I was sorry I'd fluffed the job.

"Didn't Figgis tell you about the key?"

"Figgis has gone to London," I said. "He left just before I arrived. He's staying up there."

"I see . . ." Martin's tone became slightly more amiable. "That was bad luck. Well, you'd better get his address and let us have it and we'll put someone on to him here."

"All right. What do you want me to do afterwards?"

"Stay down there, I should think, and try to get a good follow-up. Hold on a minute . . ." There was a buzz of talk, and I caught the sound of Blair's peevish pre-conference voice. "Yes—Mr. Blair says keep at it."

"You mean I'm still expected to look for the stone?"

"I imagine so. It's up to you to do what you think best, Curtis—it's your story." There was a click, and the line went dead.

I walked across to Rose Cottage in a very jaundiced frame of mind and got Figgis's address from his wife. I also asked her about the missing key. Naturally, now that the information was no longer of any use to me she remembered the incident perfectly. She even remembered how it had happened. Apparently there'd been a particularly ghastly motor smash that day, on the main road just above the castle, and her husband had heard it and gone rushing up to the road leaving the castle unattended, and it was while he was away that the key had been taken. As to who had taken it, she had absolutely no idea. In fact, it turned out that she couldn't add a thing to what Mollie had already written. That seemed to leave me at a dead end. The only thing I could think of was to go up to the castle and have another look round, and I asked her if I could borrow the key again. She said that the other reporter, the young lady, had already borrowed it, and I remembered then about Mollie's sketching. I went back to the pub and rang the News Desk and gave them Figgis's address—though I couldn't imagine what good they thought it would be—and then I strolled up to the castle. There was a new Sunbeam Talbot 90 parked outside the tea-room, a very lush job in cream and sage, obviously Mollie's, and I wondered just how many thousands a year the *Courier* paid their spoiled darling. Enough, obviously, to make her fight tooth-and-nail against all comers—even beginners!

I walked up the field path with reluctantly eager steps. She'd probably be patronising about my poor performance, which would be hard to take—yet I badly wanted to see her again.

She was sitting on a chunk of fallen masonry in the courtyard, with a sketching-block on a small folding easel in front of her. She was wearing a blouse and skirt—a pink blouse, which I would have expected to clash with her hair, though somehow it didn't. The tranquil scene, with Mollie absorbed in her work in the foreground, and the ancient grey walls of the castle in the background, made me think of some British Travel Association advertisement in a glossy American magazine. I stepped up quietly, and had a look at the sketch. It was of one of the towers, and by my standards it wasn't at all bad. She turned and greeted me with a friendly smile.

"Hallo!" she said.

"Hallo!" I said, very coldly. I'd made up my mind to be dignified and nonchalant—but I overdid it a bit.

"What happened to your story? They didn't use it, did they?"

"No."

"Too bad."

"Oh, I didn't really expect them to . . ." I stood back, and studied her drawing again with my head slightly on one side as though I were an expert, and said in an off-hand way, "I thought you did a nice piece."

"Thanks."

"Very pleasant flight of imagination, I thought."

Her beautifully plucked eyebrows became a little more arched. "Oh, not entirely."

"Haunted castle?" I said.

"All the best castles are haunted."

"Noises in the night?"

"But there have been noises. Strange knockings and clankings—most weird. Haven't you heard about them?"

"And terrified villagers?"

"Scared to death."

"The amours of Sir Bedford?"

"That's in the guide book—you shouldn't skip! And the missing key stuff is certainly true."

"Oh, that's true enough. That's why you kept quiet about it, of course!" I meant to sound teasing, but my voice came out peevish.

She looked at me in surprise. "What did you expect me to do—give you a carbon copy of my story? I paid you the compliment of supposing you'd prefer to stand on your own feet."

"Quite right. I'm merely admiring your powers of dissimulation."

"Well, all's fair in love and war, you know."

"Reporting is war, I take it?"

"To the knife! That's the whole fun of it. No quarter asked or given, survival of the fittest, and the weakest to the wall. A glorious, unscrupulous free-for-all!"

"A hard philosophy," I said.

"I don't think so. After all, no one *has* to be a reporter. If you are one, you can't afford to be squeamish. You've got to be tough—very tough—or you just won't last. You'll soon learn."

"I'm learning fast," I said.

She drew a few more lines on her sketch pad and then looked up at me again, curiously. "I believe you're really sore with me."

I managed a rather feeble grin. "I am," I said, "but I know I've no right to be. You got a damned good story and I'm envious, that's all." It wasn't quite all, but it sufficed.

"Well, that's frank," she said. "Don't worry, you'll get your break before long. . . . What are you doing around here to-day, anyway?"

"I'm supposed to be doing a follow-up."

"Is there one?"

"I wouldn't have thought so—not unless I can get a line on the chap who pinched the key."

"What makes you think he had anything to do with the stone?"

"It was you who suggested it."

"I didn't suppose anyone would take it seriously. Probably some tourist took the key as a souvenir."

"Then we're back where we were—how did the stone thief get in?"

She shook her head sadly. "Poor old *Record*!" she said, "always flogging dead horses. If you find out how he got in, the explanation will probably be quite banal. Why spoil a good mystery?"

"Don't ask me," I said, "it's not my idea. All I know is that I'm expected to produce something good—preferably the stone. I've a damn' good mind to drain the moat and charge it to expenses!"

"Now that's what I call enterprise."

"How deep is it, do you think?"

"The water's eight feet deep, according to Figgis, and there are two feet of sticky black mud at the bottom."

"Really? Oh, well, perhaps I'd better content myself with another walk round."

I wandered over to the bombard, very much aware that I was merely playing out time until the office came to its senses and recalled me. I examined the grass around the gun like a detective looking for clues. There were lots of marks, but nothing at all helpful. If there had been, I'd probably have noticed them the first time. I moved on, covering all the old ground again. I climbed down into the little dungeon, and up on to the flat roof. I poked about in the empty towers, and examined all the broken masonry that dotted the sides of the courtyard in case the thief should have left some bit of tell-tale litter behind him. But there wasn't even a

cigarette end to be seen. I found two sweet papers and an old
sardine tin in a bed of nettles, and that was all. I descended to the
basement of the well tower, but there was nothing there, either. At
least, I didn't think there was. Then I wondered. There was a lot
of soft wet mud around the well, and it had taken quite a number
of footprints. Some were mine from the previous day, some probably
were Mollie's. Some, no doubt, were Figgis's. The rest might be
the workmen's, though there was no sign of repairs here. There
were certainly three different sets of men's prints, possibly four.
Some of them went right round the well. The stone *could* have
been thrown down the well—though it seemed rather unlikely
considering how much nearer the moat was to the bombard.

If I'd been a free man, and not a hag-ridden one, I wouldn't
have given it another thought. I'd have gone and sat in the sun
with Mollie till lunchtime. But an imaginary conversation was
already running through my mind. It was six in the evening, and
I was telling Hatcher that I'd searched the castle without success
and he was saying was there a well and I was saying yes there was
and he was saying what had I done about it and I was saying
"Nothing" and he was saying then bloody well go and do something.
So I stayed and pondered, gazing down at the opaque green water.

It was a big well, at least eight feet across, surrounded by a
protective railing but uncovered. I wondered how deep it was, and
decided that I might as well find out. I returned to the courtyard,
where I'd noticed a few tools of Figgis's in an alcove. I chose a
rake, and took it back to the well and pushed it down into the
water as far as I could, but it didn't reach bottom. I'd have to tie
something else to it.

I searched among the tools for some string but there wasn't any.
Then I remembered that I'd seen a piece beside the parcel of
sketching-materials that Mollie had brought with her, and I went
over and asked her if I could borrow it. She said, "What on earth
are you up to now?"

"I'm trying to find out how deep the well is," I said.

"Ten feet. It's in the guide book."

I thanked her politely, and took the string and found a long pole in the alcove and lashed it to the rake. Then I carried the contraption to the well. After a moment Mollie put her sketch book down and joined me there.

"Muscling in?" I said.

"Just idle curiosity. Are you still looking for the stone?"

I nodded. "This seemed easier than the moat."

"You'll probably lose the rake."

I pushed the unwieldy probe down into the water till it touched bottom. Then I began to move it around, cautiously, because the lashing wasn't very secure. The bottom was soft, but after a moment or two I came up against some hard obstruction.

"You know, I believe it is here!" I exclaimed. I wiggled the pole, trying to make out the shape of the object, and it seemed to be round, and about the right size.

Mollie gave me a teasing smile. "It'll make a wonderful follow-up," she said. "I can see it now—front-page splash, streamer across seven columns. Byline—'From Our Special Correspondent, Hugh Curtis.' And then the sensational facts! 'To-day I am in a position to reveal exclusively that the stone shot believed to have been stolen from Lodden Castle was in fact dropped down a well . . .! *What a story!*"

"At least I'll be able to stop looking for the perishing thing," I said, and continued to wiggle. Mollie leaned over the rail, and helped to steady the rake.

Then suddenly, horribly, it happened. There was a stir in the water, and a lot of bubbles, and something large came swirling up to the surface and floated there.

It was the fully-dressed body of a man.

Chapter Five

For a moment we gazed down in shocked silence at the white, bloated face. Then Mollie gasped "Oh!" and turned quickly and rushed up the short flight of steps to the courtyard.

I felt a bit queasy myself, but not for long. I was much too excited. I climbed over the railing to see if I could get the body out. The water was almost level with the ground or I'd never have managed it. As it was I was able to drag it out with a bit of a struggle. It seemed to be the body of a fairly elderly man, judging by the sparse grey hair. The face, after its soaking, could have been pretty well anyone's. As I straightened the waterlogged torso, I saw that a length of stout wire had been looped round the waist, and twisted, and then formed into another loop which made a perfect circle about fifteen inches in diameter. The mystery of the stone shot, at least, was solved. It had simply been used as a weight to keep the body under water.

I wasn't quite sure what to do next, and I went up the steps to look for Mollie. She was folding up her easel. Her face was a pale shade of green, and for once the colour didn't go with her hair. She was not, I decided, with an odd feeling of relief, quite as tough as she'd pretended.

"Are you all right?" I said.

"I will be in a minute."

"It *was* pretty nasty."

"Strictly between ourselves," she said, "I never did like corpses. Particularly those that bob up under your nose without warning. . . . I suppose the stone was holding him down."

I nodded, and told her about the wire. She insisted on going down the steps again to have a look for herself. She had got over the first shock, now, and her normal colour was rapidly returning. She examined the wire with cool professional interest.

I said, "What do we do next? Search the body for some identification? I don't mind trying."

"Better not," she said. "If the police found out there'd be a frightful row—*and* we wouldn't get another thing out of them."

"In that case, I suppose we'd better go and tell them."

She nodded. "If we play along with them, we may be able to clean up the story before anyone else can get to work on it. Come on!"

There was a telephone booth near the tea-house. I asked for the headquarters of the West Sussex C.I.D. and was put through at once. It was Mollie's idea to get the big brass out quickly. I spoke to a sergeant first, and then to a chief inspector, and I told the inspector what we'd found. He said he'd be right over and asked us to stay where we were. He needn't have worried! We went back to the castle to wait for him.

Fifteen minutes later two police cars drew up at the kissing-gate and four plain-clothes men came up the path and joined us. The chief inspector introduced himself. His name was Cobley. He was a big, grim-looking man with a thin, tight mouth, but his manner to us was friendly enough.

I told him how we'd come to be there, and how I'd been poking about for the stone shot when the body had appeared. He knew about the shot, because he'd read Mollie's story in the *Courier* that morning. I told him I'd pulled the body out, and he looked a bit disapproving, but he didn't say anything. He took his sergeant down to the well, and we stood on the steps while they examined the body. After a moment Cobley felt in the inside breast pocket of the dead man's jacket and produced a wallet, which he brought out into the brighter light of the courtyard.

"Bashed on the head!" he remarked laconically to a third man. The two who had not yet seen the body went down to look. Cobley put the wallet on a bit of broken wall and opened it carefully and began to go through the sodden contents. About the first thing he pulled out was a driving licence.

"May we know who he is, inspector?" Mollie asked, in her most cajoling tone.

"I don't see why not," Cobley said. "You'll have to give us time to break the news to the relatives before you start any inquiries, that's all ... John Hoad, Down View, Clifton Road, Brighton."

I memorised the name and address.

"I'll want a statement from you two," he said. "Just hold on a minute ..."

He turned to the other men and gave them some instructions. One of them went back to the gate. Another prepared to take photographs of the body and its surroundings. The third went off for a preliminary look round the castle.

"Now then," said Cobley, "if you'd just let me have the main details again. Exactly what time was it when you found the body ...?"

I gave him the details. Mollie confirmed them. It occurred to me that he'd probably want to see Figgis some time, so I told him where the caretaker could be found in London. He made a note and thanked me for the information. Then he checked our shoes against the footprints round the well. He didn't seem very hopeful about the prints. "Looks like a herd of buffaloes has been around here," he grumbled. He had a look at the grass near the bombard, and then set off on a tour of the castle. We went with him, in case he discovered anything we'd overlooked, but he didn't appear to. That seemed to exhaust the immediate possibilities. Presently two men came up the field path with a stretcher, and the body was taken away under a rug. The photographer had all the pictures he needed, and was packing up his camera.

Cobley said, "By the way, Miss Bourne, what were those noises in the night that you mentioned in your story? Anything specific?"

Mollie avoided my eye. "Not really, Inspector. Just—well, sound effects."

"Atmosphere, eh?"

"That's all."

He nodded tolerantly. Just then, two more men came up the hill, drawing a wheeled pump behind them. They took it to the well tower and started the engine and we watched while they pumped the well dry. Afterwards one of them went down by ladder. There was nothing at the bottom but a thin layer of mud, and the stone shot.

Another man came up to Cobley and said something that I didn't catch. He turned to us. "All right," he said, "I don't think I need detain you two any longer. Thank you for your help."

Mollie smiled and said, "Thank *you*, Inspector," and we departed together. As we reached her car she said, "Well, this is where we split up."

"War to the knife again?"

"Naturally. It begins to look like quite a story."

"Why don't you get a job on the *Record*?" I said. "Then we could work together all the time."

"What do you think I am," she said, "a plumber's mate? Well—good luck!" She got into her car, and drove off as though she were leaving the pits on a race track.

She hadn't said where she was going, but I assumed it was Brighton. I wondered if I ought to ring the office and tell them what had happened, but decided that I'd better go to Brighton, too, and ring them later. The Riley was at the pub, and I hurried down and collected it.

It wasn't until I was well on my way that I began to think of the distasteful interview ahead. Even though Cobley's men had presumably taken care of the news-breaking, the widow—assuming there was one—would hardly be in much of a state to talk to reporters. In any case, Mollie would be there before me, getting all there was to get and probably queering the pitch for me. It was annoying that she'd managed to get ahead once more. I stepped hard on the accelerator. I didn't expect to catch her, but at least I wouldn't be far behind. Then, as I slowed through Worthing High Street, I suddenly saw the Sunbeam Talbot. It was drawn up beside the kerb behind a police car, and a flat-capped policeman, evidently impervious to charm, was making notes in a book. Homer, it seemed, had nodded.

I reached Brighton just after one o'clock. Clifton Road turned out to be a new one, cut out of the Downs at the edge of the town. The houses were small, detached villas, with small, trim gardens. Down View was the last house but one. I parked outside and walked up a concrete path between beds of tulips and rang the bell in some trepidation. Meeting the bereaved was going to be a good deal worse than finding a body. Expressions of sympathy, apologies for the intrusion, were already on my lips. But no one came. I rang the bell again, but now I scarcely expected anyone to come. Probably the widow had gone off with the police—they'd obviously want to question her. Or perhaps she'd gone to see the remains, poor soul!

I was just turning away, half-relieved and half-disappointed, when I heard a step on the path next door and a woman emerged from the back garden. She was elderly, with a bird's nest of grey hair and bright blue eyes. She wore a coloured smock, and she had a builder's trowel in one hand and half a brick in the other. She looked at me across the fence and said, "Are you the police again?"

I told her I was a reporter from the *Record*.

"Oh, yes. It's about poor Mr. Hoad, I suppose?"

I nodded.

"I'm afraid you won't find anyone to talk to, except me." She gave the half-brick a light tap. "I'm just building a wall. . . . Mrs. Hoad's up in Scotland, visiting her mother. Dear, oh dear, what a shocking business. I could scarcely believe it when they told me."

She looked moderately upset, but at least a neighbour's distress was manageable. And she was obviously quite prepared to talk. I said, "Do you happen to know Mrs. Hoad's address in Scotland?"

"It's a place called Inveraray, that's all I know. I told the police and they said they'd be able to find her. I can hardly bear to think about it—it's going to be such a dreadful shock for her."

"It's bound to be," I said sympathetically, and moved closer to the fence. "A ghastly thing to have happened! It was I who found Mr. Hoad's body, you know. I've just come from the place."

"Have you really? They say someone hit him on the head—was that what happened?"

"Apparently." She seemed avid for detail, so I gave her some. She lapped it up.

"Well, I just can't imagine how anyone could have done such a thing to him," she said at last. "He was such a nice, quiet man—he wouldn't have hurt a fly himself. I'm sure he never did anyone any harm. There really are some very wicked people in the world."

I agreed. "How old would you say he was?" I asked. "Sixty?"

"Oh, not as much as that—more like fifty. His wife is much younger—Norah, her name is. She's only about thirty—she's very pretty."

"Have they any family?"

"A little boy of four. He's up with his mother in Scotland. Poor little chap . . ."

"Have you any idea what Mr. Hoad could have been doing at Lodden?" I asked.

"Why, yes, he was on his boat," she said, as though she thought I knew. "It was one of his favourite spots, the river there. He was having a week's holiday, you see, while his wife was away."

"What sort of boat is it?"

"Well, I don't know exactly, I've never seen it—I think it's just an ordinary boat, with an engine. It was his hobby, he was absolutely mad about it. Mrs. Hoad didn't like going on the sea because it always made her ill, but she often joined him for a week-end on the river when the weather was nice—and the little boy too, of course. They were all absolutely devoted to each other. Such a tragedy!"

"Terrible!" I said. "Do you happen to know the name of the boat?"

"Now let me think—it was some bird. *Snipe*, that's it."

I nodded. "What did Mr. Hoad do for a living?"

"He was a chartered accountant."

"Did he go up to town every day?"

"No, he worked here in Brighton."

"Had he many friends?"

"Oh, yes, a great many. Everybody liked him."

"Well, there must have been one person who didn't," I said. I thanked her for the information she'd given me, and asked her for her own name, which was Prew. Miss Prew, I gathered. Then I left. As I turned into the main road, Mollie turned out of it. She made a face at me as she passed.

I popped into a pub and had a beer and a sandwich, and then I rang the office. Lawson was on the Desk.

I said, "This is Curtis. I thought I'd better let you know that I've found a body in a well."

There was a moment's silence. Then Lawson said, anxiously, "Are you drunk, old boy?"

"Sober as a judge," I assured him. "Remember that stone shot I was looking for?—it was tied to the body. The police have just taken the chap away."

"Christ!" he said. "Look, hold on—I'd better tell Blair. He's up in the canteen."

I held on. In a moment or two, Blair came on the phone, a bit breathless. "Hallo, Curtis," he said. "What's all this about a body?"

I told him. He kept grunting encouragingly—he had a most eager grunt when he was hearing news of a story. He seemed very pleased.

"Well, it sounds like a first-class story," he said. "Is anyone else on to it yet?"

"Mollie Bourne," I said.

"Oh!" A little of the excitement went out of his voice; a hint of anxiety came into it. "Have you put your story over yet?"

"No, but I can in a few minutes."

"I think you'd better, Curtis—I'd like to know the strength of it. Let's have it quickly—everything you've got. After that you'd better get back to the castle—but keep in touch." He was as nervous and fussy as an old aunt. I said I would, and he rang off.

I wrote out the story—I still didn't trust myself to dictate a piece straight over the phone from notes. I wrote it straight, in the first person, just as it had happened, with all the facts I knew and the interview with Miss Prew at the end. It sounded pretty good to me as I phoned it. I had another word with Lawson and then drove back to London.

Things had changed a lot at the castle by the time I got there. A dozen cars were parked beside the kissing-gate and the place was swarming with reporters. Most of them, I was glad to find, had only just arrived. P.C. Mathers was on guard at the gate, moving on local sightseers with a mixture of embarrassment and self-importance. Inside the castle a couple of plain-clothes men were at work again, carefully hoisting the stone shot out of the well. Apparently there was some hope of fingerprints, even though it had been under water. A man was watching them whom I hadn't seen before, and he turned out to be Tom Figgis. The police had got in touch with him in London and he'd come straight down. He was a strongly-built, dark-haired man of thirty or so, with cold blue eyes and more assurance than I'd have expected in a countryman. His voice was clear and emphatic, with almost nothing of the local burr about it, and I could imagine him as an excellent guide. He wasn't very forthcoming when I tackled him, perhaps because he'd already been interviewed by the police and all the other reporters, but he opened out a bit when I told him it was I who'd found the body. The only trouble was, he didn't know anything, except what had already come out.

I hung about for a while, but nothing fresh emerged and I didn't think anything was likely to. About four I went back to the Castle Arms, and there was a message for me to ring the office. This time I got straight through to Blair.

"Oh, hallo, Curtis," he said, in a voice that was almost genial. "That's a very good piece you sent, very good indeed. We'll certainly be using some of it. The Editor's very pleased with it."

"I'm glad about that," I murmured.

"Now look, Curtis, we're sending Lawson down to take over. I don't want you to think it's any reflection on you, you've done very well, but it's an important story and it needs a man of experience. So Lawson will be down early this evening, and I'd like you to work under his direction."

"Very well," I said.

"In the meantime, will you try to get a line on that boat of Hoad's—it must be somewhere around. You might find some clue, there—and anyway, we'd like a description of it. We've got a good start on this, and we've got to keep ahead."

"I'll do my best," I said.

"Good! That's all, then." Blair gave a little chuckle into the phone. "We'll make a reporter of you yet, Curtis!"

Chapter Six

I put the receiver down with mixed feelings. Blair's praise had fallen on my ears like music, and the fact that I'd done reasonably well so far made it all the harder to accept gracefully the fact that I was to be superseded. All the same, I realised that Blair was probably right. I'd had a lot of luck up till now, but at any moment I might find myself out of my depth. From the *Record's* point of view, Lawson was a much safer proposition.

Meanwhile, I still had an hour or two on my own before he arrived, and I resolved to make the most of it. First I went back to the castle to see if I could pick up any news of the boat there, but the detectives had gone and Figgis, as usual, knew nothing. Mathers, still on duty at the gate, told me Inspector Cobley was setting up his temporary headquarters at the police station in Worley, a small market town about five miles from Lodden, so I drove straight over. But the plain-clothes men were all out on the job, and the station sergeant hadn't heard about any boat. It looked as though I should have to conduct my own search. I bought an inch-to-the-mile map of the district and studied the course of the River Lod. There were only about seven miles of it between the sea and the castle, and I knew Hoad couldn't have cruised above the castle because the road bridge at Lodden was too low to get under. Seven miles didn't seem too formidable a proposition. I debated whether it would be quicker to make hit-or-miss inquiries at various points along the route, or to cover the whole distance myself on foot. In the end, I decided to walk it.

I drove back to Lodden, parked the car, and set off southwards along the river bank. There was no proper path, but the river ran mainly through quiet pastures and I didn't think anyone would object to my doing a bit of trespassing. During the next half hour I waded through several patches of mud, climbed a lot of fences, and scrambled through some very prickly hedges. It was warm work, for the sky was cloudless and the sun still beat down fiercely. Once I heard the sound of a tractor in the distance, and I saw plenty of sheep and cows, but no people. I passed two pleasure boats, moored to the bank beside farm tracks, but this was a week-day and they were both unoccupied. There was no sign at all of *Snipe*.

I'd walked about three miles when, from somewhere not far ahead, I caught the unmistakable sound of a two-stroke engine, and a moment later a small boat appeared round a bend in the river, travelling fast. It was a light dinghy, driven by an outboard motor. There were two men in it. By the time I'd identified one of them as Inspector Cobley it had swept past me and disappeared round another bend.

I felt pretty sure they were looking for *Snipe*. If they'd stopped I could have saved them a journey. As it was, they'd saved me one. There was obviously no point now in going on, so I sat down on the bank to rest and wait for the dinghy's return. It looked, after all, as though I shouldn't be able to add much to my story. I wondered what Mollie was doing, and how she'd got on with the slightly eccentric Miss Prew. Maybe, I thought, she wasn't so good with elderly spinsters as she was with susceptible men.

Twenty minutes passed, and then I heard the outboard again. As the dinghy approached within hailing distance I cupped my hands and called out, "No sign of *Snipe*?" This time Cobley recognised me. He slowed for a moment and shook his head. "Not on this river!" he shouted. Then he opened up again, and they were gone.

I sat on for a while, pondering. If Hoad hadn't been killed near the castle, how had the murderer got his body to the well? If he had been killed near the castle, I'd have expected his boat to be somewhere around. The mystery seemed to be deepening. But without any information to go on it was idle to speculate, and presently I got up and began to retrace my steps back towards Lodden.

There was a strong smell of petrol in the air, and I noticed that the outboard had left a slick of oil on the water. It drifted slowly downstream, a patch of irridescent purple and green. A couple of hundred yards ahead there was another patch. For the next half mile there were patches at regular intervals. Cobley's engine evidently needed attention. Then, right before my eyes, a stretch of water that had been clear suddenly became covered with the same oily colours. The oil *wasn't* from the outboard! It was coming up from the river bed. It must have been coming up when I'd passed by before, only I'd been too busy thinking about *Snipe* then to notice.

I watched the spot, fascinated. The patch of oil drifted away on the lazy current. The water cleared. Several minutes went by. Then a bubble rose to the surface and broke and the water was oily again.

I took off my shoes and socks and rolled up my trousers and stepped down into the river. The water was cold, but not too cold. I started to wade out, but the sides shelved too sharply. The channel in the middle must be eight or ten feet deep. If I was going to investigate, I should have to swim.

I climbed out and considered the situation. There was undoubtedly something under the water that was leaking petrol. It might be a not-quite-empty tin that someone had thrown in. It certainly didn't have to be *Snipe*. On the other hand, it could be. If it was, it would round off my day's work splendidly, and I should have the find to myself. It wouldn't take more than a moment or two to make sure, and I could dry off in the sun. I took a quick look round. Except for a small clump of trees just ahead of me there were open fields on all sides, and there was no one about. I stripped off my clothes and slid into the water.

Half a dozen strokes brought me to the middle of the river, and I dived cautiously. The water was remarkably clear. I looked ahead, and almost at once I saw a large object sitting on the river bed. It *was* the boat! It was almost upright, and the top of the cabin was about four feet under water. I surfaced for air and then swam down again and made a circuit of the boat. It had a brown hull, and it was about twenty feet long. As I rounded the stern I saw that one of the planks had come away from its fastenings. The woodwork was badly smashed, and not by accident, for there were deep round marks as though it had been hit with some heavy instrument like a hammer head. It was pretty clear that *Snipe* had been scuttled.

I surfaced again, and climbed on to the cabin top, and stood up with the top half of me out of the water. As I emerged I heard a sharp cry from the bank and turned quickly. It was Mollie. She'd just come out from the trees, and she was gazing at me in utter astonishment.

"What on earth are you standing on?" she said.

It was much too late to pretend I was treading water. I said, "Father, I cannot tell a lie. I'm standing on someone's old boat."

"Why?"

"Well, mainly because I've nothing on. Nudity without reciprocity always strikes me as rather undignified."

She smiled, but only for a moment. Her glance switched to a patch of oil that was just drifting away.

"It can't be a *very* old boat," she said. "Is it *Snipe*?"

"You surely don't expect me to give you a carbon copy of my story?" I said.

"You might at least tell me if it's *Snipe*."

I grinned. "I don't seem to remember anything in your professional code about an armistice. War to the knife, you said—nothing about flags of truce."

"I think you're being most objectionable."

"Oh, I'm not insisting on my rights—I don't mind putting you in the picture. The fact is, I've found an old Norwegian burial ship. It's about fifty feet long, and it's full of treasure. Quite a discovery!"

"I suppose I'll have to come and look," she said coldly, and turned towards the wood.

I called after her. "Don't be silly—I don't mind telling you. Always ready to help a colleague in trouble!"

"Thanks, but I don't think I want my news second-hand, after all. How do I know you'd tell me the truth?"

"Just as you like," I said. "In that case I'll see you in the water—I hope!"

I rested a bit longer, and then dived in again. I wanted to have a look in the cabin if I could, but the doors were shut and by the time I'd got them open I needed air again. I reached the surface just in time to see Mollie approaching from up-stream at a fast crawl. I caught the flash of a gleaming shoulder, and then she dived. I waited a moment, and went in after her. She was just disappearing round the stern. I turned in the opposite direction and she swam past me, a yard away, white and graceful. She looked much more attractive than any mermaid. I went on till I was over the cockpit and swam down and peered through the cabin doors. I don't know what I'd expected to find there, but there was nothing of any obvious interest. Perhaps I just wasn't concentrating. I surfaced for the last time and swam back to my clothes. I dried off as well as I could with a pocket handkerchief, and dressed damply. Mollie was already on her way back upstream to the wood.

She emerged a few minutes later, combed and lip-sticked, though hardly her usual *soignée* self. She gave me an amused smile.

"Well," she said, "satisfied?"

"I wouldn't say that."

"The things I do for my paper!"

"You owed it to them," I said. I wanted to ask her if she'd noticed the broken plank, but I didn't, in case she hadn't.

"Well, we'd better be getting back," she said. "If we phone our stories first, and tell the police about it afterwards, there's a chance we'll beat the others to the first editions."

It was after seven when we reached the Castle Arms. I decided to try dictating my addition without writing it, as it was a simple descriptive piece, and I got through it quite well. I reported the new development to Blair, who grunted happily and said, "Splendid, Curtis!" Then, as I left the box, I ran into Lawson. He'd just checked in at the reception desk.

"Hallo, old boy!" he said affably. "I say, I hope you don't mind me butting in like this?"

"Of course not," I lied.

"Personally," he said, with equal insincerity, "I'd have left you to handle it on your own as you were doing so well, but you know what an old woman Blair is. Anyway, it'll probably take both of us to exploit the thing properly."

I nodded; and he looked relieved. "Let's go and have a drink, then," he said, "and you can fill me in on what's happened." He grinned. "You certainly did run slap into this story, didn't you? Quite a break!"

"Just beginner's luck," I said modestly.

Chapter Seven

I had all the papers sent up to my room next morning, and for the first time I had the exquisite pleasure of seeing myself in print and my name over a story. The *Record* had really done me very well. What I'd sent had been subbed down to about half its original length, but I'd made the front page, and my first-person descriptions of finding the body and the boat were more or less intact.

I read Mollie's story next—and once again I had a slight feeling of chagrin. She'd done a first-person account, too, but with a difference. I'd described how "I and another reporter" had found the body. She'd just said "I," and she'd conveyed to her readers an impression of great resource and efficiency in dealing with a peculiarly horrible situation. There was no doubt that Mollie had a flair for getting her personality across in her pieces—which I supposed was what she was paid for. She'd managed to get more atmosphere in, too, which made her story very effective, and of course she'd had the advantage of being able to follow up her own piece of the previous day.

Still, when I looked at my story again—and I did it at pretty frequent intervals during the next few hours—I decided that I'd no cause for dissatisfaction. If Mollie had the edge on me, I certainly had more than the edge on everybody else. Thanks to her delaying tactics, none of the other reporters had had time to check up on the boat.

I met her in the lobby on my way down to breakfast. She was wearing a thin tweed suit that I hadn't seen before and she looked very smart. To my male eye, at any rate, her beautifully waving hair bore little trace of the soaking it had had in the river. She looked, I thought, more like a photographer's model than a working reporter.

I said, "Morning, Mollie!"

"Morning!" she said brightly.

"I've just been reading your story. I thought that was a pretty good effort of yours, dealing with the body single-handed. Some women would have been too upset!"

For once, it seemed to me that her self-possession faltered. In fact, I believed I detected a very faint blush.

"I didn't write it like that," she said. "The subs. altered it."

I grinned. "I believe you," I said, "but millions wouldn't."

"Cross my heart!"

"Well, it read very nicely, anyway. I don't know how you do it."

"Your piece was good, too," she said graciously. "The trouble with you is that you're too modest—you've got to put yourself over in this game, it's like show business. 'I' did this, and 'I' did that—I'm the great reporter offering you this wonderful story—that is, of course, when the story will stand it. Blow yourself up! Present yourself! Give the impression you're some sort of superman!"

"I'd feel damn' silly."

"Why? There's no need to take the nonsense seriously. You don't suppose I really care whether two million people think I found a body or not. It's just part of the racket."

"You baffle me," I said.

"What's baffling about me?"

"You look such a nice girl!"

"God!" she said, and went in to breakfast.

The dining-room was packed with reporters. Lawson was there, reading the papers over his coffee. He congratulated me warmly on my story, but he seemed a bit puzzled. "Are you and Mollie Bourne running some sort of co-operative society?" he asked.

"On the contrary," I said, "we're at each other's throats."

"I just wondered. It's odd she should have noticed that petrol on the water, too. Pretty chancy thing to happen."

"She's a very observant girl," I said.

"She certainly is—she even spotted the smashed hull." He was

43

silent a moment. "She must have been swimming around with nothing on, too. Wish I'd been there."

"I bet you do!" I said.

He still looked faintly suspicious, but he didn't pursue the subject. I poured some coffee, and asked him what the orders were for the day. He said we couldn't do much until we got the basic facts from the police, and that for the moment the best thing was to stick around with him. About ten we went off along the river bank to watch them raising *Snipe*. They'd brought some experts along, and the whole job only took about an hour. They brought her to the bank to dry out, and after they'd had a preliminary look round we were allowed aboard one at a time, with instructions not to touch. Actually, there was nothing very interesting there. The cabin, in spite of its soaking, bore all the marks of occupation by a methodical, boat-proud owner. The sleeping-bag was carefully rolled, the stove had obviously been kept spotlessly clean. There was a fishing-rod and a portable radio and a paper-backed novel or two—everything to suggest a pleasant, carefree holiday, nothing to hint at violence. It didn't look as though the boat itself had played any part in the murder—except to carry the unfortunate victim nearer to the scene.

When Cobley left, just before twelve, we went along with him to his headquarters and more or less camped out there until well into the afternoon, collecting scraps of information as they appeared. For the first time I had a chance of seeing Lawson at work, and it was quite an education. He undoubtedly had a way with him where policemen were concerned, which was probably why he was a Crime Reporter. I don't quite know how he did it, but he seemed able to insinuate himself into their confidence with enviable ease. It wasn't just that his name was known to them, because that applied to a lot of the other reporters as well. Perhaps it was his "old boy" approach and his total lack of "side" that won them over. Anyway, he was soon on excellent terms with Cobley's sergeant and with most of the other plain-clothes men, and though he didn't actually prise away any facts that our rivals didn't get, I could well imagine him doing so.

There was very little for me to do. Figgis called at the station just before lunch and I had a few words with him, but he still didn't know anything. Afterwards I saw Lawson in smiling conversation with him. Lawson, it seemed, could get on with anyone.

About three that afternoon we had an informal press conference with Cobley and he told us what the police had discovered so far. It didn't amount to a great deal. Hoad had been killed, it appeared, by two savage blows from some blunt instrument, possibly a cosh. If something heavier had been used, it had probably been wrapped up in a cloth of some kind, because though the skull had been fractured the skin had scarcely been broken and there had been almost no blood. The murder had been committed two nights ago. Hoad had been noticed by a farmer, cruising up river about four miles below the castle, at around six in the evening, which was the last time anyone but the murderer had seen him alive. At that time, the stone shot had been in place; by nine next morning it had disappeared. The official view seemed to be that Hoad had probably continued on his way to the castle, tied up near there for the night, and been killed somewhere close by. The wire that had been used to make the stone fast to him might well have been aboard the boat, though that was speculation. The murderer, having disposed of the body, had then brought the boat downstream where the water was deeper and scuttled it, presumably in the hope that when both Hoad and *Snipe* were reported missing it would be supposed that he had put out to sea again and met with some accident there.

The only indication of motive—and this came as a surprise—was that something like twenty pounds in notes was missing from Hoad's wallet. According to his bank, he'd drawn that amount for his week's holiday, and it seemed very unlikely that he could have spent more than a fraction of it. The case might therefore be a comparatively simple one of robbery with lethal violence, unplanned and fortuitous. There was no other known reason why anyone should have wanted to kill Hoad. As far as could be gathered, he had been a worthy citizen in every way—a conscientious worker, a kind husband and father, a man with many friends and no enemies.

At the same time, Cobley admitted, there was no present explanation of how a casual murderer could have got into the castle, and the police were still looking into this. If the murder hadn't been casual, but premeditated, then it was possible that the theft of the castle key four years earlier might have something to do with it. And that, for the moment, was all. Questions, Cobley said, would have to be postponed until later.

It wasn't a very satisfying statement, but it gave us a certain amount of copy to be going on with. We drove quickly back to the pub, and Lawson phoned half a column off the cuff. Then he joined me in the lounge. I'd been thinking quite a bit about what Cobley had told us, and the more I thought about it the more snags I could see.

I said, "What do you think about this casual murder idea?"

He grinned. "Not much, old boy. And I'd lay long odds that Cobley doesn't, either."

"He made quite a point of it."

"Oh, he wants it published, all right—but that doesn't mean he believes it. He may be trying to lull the real murderer. False sense of security, that sort of thing. Or he may just be covering up in advance in case he can't find a better explanation."

"Do the police do that?"

"You bet they do! There's nothing like having a passing tramp to put the blame on if no one else turns up. . . . But in this case, of course, it's just nonsense. You could hardly have anything less casual than the way that body and boat were disposed of."

"That's what I thought," I said. "All the same, I suppose some thug *might* have done the job on the spur of the moment and then realised it would be safer to get rid of the traces?"

"Don't you believe it, old boy. He'd have left the body where it fell and cleared off with the twenty quid—he wouldn't have hung about for hours fooling with boats. Why should he, if he had no connection with Hoad? Whoever went to all that trouble must have had a damned good reason—and if you ask me, it was because he knew that if the murder was uncovered it would be linked with him."

"Where do you think the twenty pounds comes in?"

Lawson shrugged. "Maybe the murderer took the money as a blind. . . . It's an old dodge. Or perhaps it was an afterthought—why pass up twenty quid when it's there for the taking . . .? Mind you, it's *just* possible he knew Hoad had the money on him and did the whole thing for that—but somehow I can't see it. I'd say it was a carefully planned job by someone who badly wanted to get rid of him."

I nodded. So far we were seeing eye to eye. "All right," I said, "let's suppose the murderer had a personal motive. Let's suppose the whole thing was premeditated. Where does that get us? It seems wildly unlikely to me that someone stole the castle key four years ago with the intention of bumping Hoad off on the premises four years later. And if it wasn't stolen for that reason, why was it stolen? And if the murderer didn't use the stolen key, how did he get in?"

Lawson said, "What do you think I am, old boy, an electronic brain . . .? Still, I don't mind having a bash. In the first place, how do we know a key was stolen?"

I stared at him. "Well, surely . . .?"

"Figgis says it was, but we've only got his word for it."

Oddly enough, I'd never thought of that. After a moment, I said, "Well, can't it be checked? He must have reported it to the castle people at the time."

"He didn't, old boy. I asked him this morning."

"Really . . .? Did he say why not?"

"He said he had another key so it didn't seem worth making a fuss about."

"Well, that could be true, I suppose."

"It could—and it could be untrue. In our game, you can't be too suspicious."

I said, "Do you mean you suspect Figgis of the murder?"

"Between you and me and the gatepost, old boy, I'd say it was a possibility. Who's the man who'd be linked at once with any murder at the castle? Figgis! And who had the opportunity to commit the murder? Figgis! He had a key, he could have slipped out of his house at night, knowing that Hoad's boat was already moored near the castle, he could have done the job. And as far as we know, no one else could. He'd realise that, too. So what would he do? Invent a stolen key story to provide an alternative. I think it all fits rather well."

I suddenly remembered my talk with Mrs. Figgis. I said, "But his wife told me about the key. She gave me a most circumstantial account of how it came to be lost."

"She may be in it, too!"

I gaped. The way he was scything down people's characters was quite staggering.

"I'm glad *my* reputation isn't in your hands," I said.

He eyed me quizzically. "Don't be too sure it isn't, old boy."

I knew that in another moment he'd have worked the conversation round to Mollie again. He had a single-track mind, with just a few sidings for crime. I said hurriedly, "Well, I think you're jumping to a lot of conclusions. What about the stone shot? Surely Figgis, of all people, wouldn't have wanted to draw attention to the castle by using that?"

"Perhaps there wasn't anything else."

I cast my mind back to the castle. There was a lot of broken masonry, but I couldn't recall any loose bits. "Still, he could have taken something in with him," I said.

"It's a point," Lawson admitted.

"Anyway, what reason could Figgis have had? I certainly can't see him killing anyone for twenty pounds—even if he'd known about it. He's got a good job, and his prospects seem even better. As for a personal motive, there's no evidence that he even knew Hoad."

"Not yet, there isn't," Lawson said, "but we may be able to find some. It's amazing what you can dig up when you try. After all, we know Hoad was up this river quite often in his boat. He probably looked in at the castle each time. He probably ran into Figgis. They may have known each other intimately by now."

"It's the purest speculation," I said.

"Of course it is, but what's wrong with that? It's our job to speculate. We've sent the basic facts—now we start on the theories."

"But surely we can't print stuff like this—so what's the point?"

"We print what we can, old boy, and we give the police what we can't. That keeps them sweet. Anyway, Blair always likes to have the low-down on a story even if it can't be used. Makes him feel important in conference!"

"Well," I said, "you're the boss. What do you suggest we do about it?"

He shrugged. "Check up on Figgis, I guess. Look into his movements lately. We might walk up to Rose Cottage for a start and see if we can find anyone who heard him sneaking out of his house on the night of the murder."

"Are you serious?"

"Why not?"

"Well, I can give you one reason—if Figgis finds out he'll probably knock your block off!"

"That's all right, old boy—you look like a pretty good bodyguard to me. Anyway, he won't know what we've been after—I always wrap these inquiries up."

As it happened, this was one time when he didn't have to. He didn't even have a chance to ask any questions. Next door to Rose Cottage there was another thatched house—Lavender Cottage. An old countryman was leaning over the front gate, smoking his pipe. A large mongrel dog sat at his feet. As we approached, the dog sprang up and began to bark at us. I looked down the path, and there was a kennel near the back door.

I said, "Good evening!" and stopped. "Does she bark like that at everyone?"

"Most everyone," he said. "She's a noisy bitch. No harm in her, though."

"Would she bark if she heard a neighbour prowling about in the night?"

He gave me an odd look. "She would that."

"Did she bark the night that man was murdered at the castle?"

The man took his pipe out of his mouth. "No," he said. "Why should she?"

"I just wondered." I took Lawson's arm and steered him back down the hill. "Now what price Figgis?" I said.

He was quite unabashed. "Let's call it 'Not Proven,' old boy," he said. "I never did trust bitches."

Chapter Eight

By next morning, though, Lawson's interest had switched to something quite different. Several papers, including the *Record*, carried an agency photograph of Hoad's widow, taken as she was about to start her long journey home from Inveraray. Even though her face in the picture was set and expressionless, it was clear that Miss Prew's description of her as "pretty" was an understatement. She was, in fact, an extremely striking brunette, and she had an excellent figure. Lawson was most impressed.

"Quite a tasty dish," he said reflectively. "We might do a lot worse than check up on Mrs. Hoad."

"*Now* what's the idea?" I said.

"Well, you know what they say, old boy—*cherchez la femme!* And here she is in the flesh—and how! It's a classic set-up, after all—attractive young wife, elderly husband. Maybe there's a lover somewhere around."

The reaper was at work again! I said, "Lawson, you're incorrigible."

"Well, we can't afford to leave any stones unturned. Come on, let's get cracking, we've got a busy day ahead."

We called first at Cobley's headquarters to see if there were any new developments, but there weren't. Then we drove to Brighton. I couldn't imagine how Lawson proposed to start his inquiries. It seemed unlikely that Mrs. Hoad had got back yet, and even if she had he could scarcely call and ask her if she had a lover. He couldn't even hope to get anything out of Miss Prew on those lines. The whole enterprise struck me as most unpromising, as well as unsavoury.

However, my education was to be carried a good deal farther that day. Lawson didn't attempt any direct inquiries. He had a talk with the milkman who was delivering up Clifton Road. He told him who we were, and said that we were trying to get a line on all the people Hoad had known but of course we couldn't ask Mrs. Hoad herself because she obviously wouldn't want to talk now, and the milkman quite saw that. Then Lawson asked him if Mrs. Hoad had had anyone to help in the house, and the milkman said, yes, she had a woman named Bray who came every morning. He didn't know where Mrs. Bray lived, except that it was on a council estate.

That was all Lawson needed. We whipped off to the town hall and Lawson went in alone. He was inside for about half an hour, and when he came out he had the addresses of two families named Bray. The first one we called at turned out to be the right one, and Mrs. Bray was at home. She was a woman of about forty, plump and pleasant but not outstandingly bright. She seemed rather flattered at being visited by two reporters, and asked us in. She told us that her husband was a bus conductor and that she had three children at school all day, which was why she'd been able to work for poor Mrs. Hoad, though she didn't know what would happen now. We all agreed that it was a dreadful thing, and Lawson said the newspapers could often help in bringing a murderer to book, and asked her if she knew of anyone that Mr. Hoad had been on bad terms with and she said she didn't. Lawson's manner conveyed the impression that that was really all he'd come about, and that anything else was just casual chatting. He asked her what Mrs. Hoad was like to work for and what the little boy was like and said he supposed when Mrs Hoad went out she left the boy with Mrs. Bray and Mrs. Bray said yes, she did, sometimes for the whole day. Lawson asked her if Mrs. Hoad had spent a whole day out lately and Mrs. Bray said she'd been up to London about a week ago. Lawson said, "Shopping, I suppose?" and Mrs. Bray said, no, she'd gone up to have lunch with a friend, and for the first time she began to look a bit uneasy about the way she was being pumped. Then Lawson made a hypocritical little speech saying he naturally didn't want Mrs. Bray to give away any secrets but of course Mrs. Hoad herself wouldn't be in a fit state to be questioned and it was really a kindness not to bring her into it but at the same time the only way poor Mr. Hoad's murderer could be found was to check up on all the people who knew the family. Then Mrs. Bray said she'd heard Mrs. Hoad making the lunch date on the telephone, and it was someone called Stanley she'd been talking to, in London, and though she couldn't be sure what Stanley it was there was a Mr. Fairfax whose name was Stanley and who was a friend of the family and belonged to some sort of boat club at Saltwater that Mr. Hoad belonged to as well, so perhaps it was him because he did work in London though he lived in Brighton. Lawson continued to plug away for a while, asking about other people that Mrs. Hoad knew, but Stanley Fairfax was the only one who seemed to offer anything. In the end he thanked Mrs. Bray, and said she'd been a great help, and we left.

By now Lawson had his nose to the trail like a bloodhound. We had a quick lunch, and then drove over to the Saltwater Yacht Club, which was at the mouth of a small river not far along the coast. There were two or three members at work on their boats, but Lawson said they'd probably be stuffy about answering questions, and after we'd looked round a bit he found a man named Sharpley who had a small boatyard alongside the club and did a lot of work for members and knew them all. Sharpley was quite willing to talk. He confirmed that Hoad had been a very pleasant man who had lots of friends and wasn't at all the sort of chap to make enemies. Lawson said he understood that one of his friends had been a Mr. Fairfax, and Sharpley said that was so and that Mr. Fairfax had accompanied the Hoads on their trips on many occasions in his own boat, *Water Baby*—though not very often lately. Lawson asked him what Fairfax was like, and Sharpley said he was a big, good-looking man of about thirty-five. By profession, he was a stockbroker, and pretty well-to-do.

That was all Lawson needed for the moment. As we left the boatyard he said, "Well, it's building up nicely, old boy, isn't it?"

I grinned. "So was Figgis!"

"Oh, we've not necessarily finished with Figgis yet. But this hangs together much better—no snags at all, so far."

"Not much substance, either," I said.

"I wouldn't say that. Why would an attractive girl nip up to town to lunch alone with a handsome young friend of her husband's if there wasn't anything between them? After all, she could have seen him down here any time. There's no smoke without fire, you know."

"Are you seriously suggesting that these two may have conspired together to get rid of the husband?"

"Why not, old boy? It wouldn't be the first time such a thing's happened, would it? Look—what about this for a reconstruction? Norah Hoad marries old Hoad for security, the way young girls often do, and then she gets bored with him. She meets this good-looking chap Fairfax four years ago and they fall for each other in a big way. They want to marry, and they can't see Hoad agreeing to a divorce, so they decide to make away with him. On one of their joint sailing trips, which happens to be up the Lod, they hit on the idea of the castle as a nice quiet place to do the job. With the well for hiding the body in, and the river for scuttling *Snipe*, they think they can make it look like an accident. Fairfax pinches the key, and bides his time. No opportunity presents itself, so in the end Norah makes it by going off to Scotland and suggesting to Hoad that he should have a week's cruise on his own. Fairfax waits for him at the castle and bumps him off according to plan. Now they're just lying low until the shouting dies, and then they'll get married. How's that for a theory?"

I said, "Apart from anything else, Mrs. Hoad was having Hoad's child about four years ago. She must have been rather occupied."

"How do we know it was Hoad's child?" Lawson said. "It could have been Fairfax's. You have to keep an open mind on these things, old boy."

I was speechless.

"Anyway," he said, "it's worth while seeing what Fairfax has to say about it."

"You don't mean that?"

"Of course."

"Then you're certainly going to need a bodyguard this time!"

"I don't think so," he said. "Just leave it to uncle!"

We looked up Stanley Fairfax in the phone book and found his address. Then we stooged around, waiting for him to get back from work. Around seven-fifteen we went along to the address. It was a big block of luxury flats, and Fairfax lived on the fifth floor. We asked the porter if he'd come in, and the porter said he had. We went up and rang the bell and Fairfax opened the door himself. He was a strongly-built, bluff looking man, with a tanned face and very blue eyes.

Lawson said, "Mr. Fairfax?"

"Yes."

"We're from the *Daily Record*." Lawson gave our names. "It's about the death of Mr. Hoad. We wondered if you could spare us a few minutes?"

Fairfax looked closely at each of us in turn, and glanced at his watch. "I suppose so," he said, "though it'll have to be a very few minutes—I'm expecting someone for dinner. Come in, will you?" He led the way into his sitting-room. "Now, what can I do for you?"

"We understand you were a friend of Mr. Hoad's?" Lawson said.

"Yes, indeed. I've known him for years. Shocking business!"

Lawson said, "The thing is, sir, everyone tells us that Mr. Hoad had no enemies, and yet someone killed him. . . . Of course, it's up to the police to find out who did it, but the newspapers are naturally concerned too, and the *Record* thought it might be a good idea to visit everyone who had any contact with the family and see if that helped at all. Naturally we don't want to trouble Mrs. Hoad at such a time . . ."

Fairfax nodded. "Well, I'd be only too glad to help, but there's nothing I can suggest. You can be sure I've thought about it a good deal myself—and I'm utterly baffled."

"Didn't he have any trouble at all, with anyone?"

"If he did, I never heard of it."

Lawson appeared to hesitate. "There was one bit of information we got, sir . . ." He broke off. "You'll understand that it's a little difficult to mention these things, particularly to a friend of the family—I don't suppose for a minute there's anything in it—but we gathered Mrs. Hoad lunched with some man in London last week. There seems to be a bit of a mystery about it—we wondered if by any chance he could be connected with the case in some way, and if you could suggest who he was."

Fairfax stared at him. Lawson gazed back guilelessly. I tried to look like a competent bodyguard.

Fairfax said, "Is this some sort of gag?"

"I'm afraid I don't know what you mean, sir . . ."

"Do you really not know who the man was?"

"Indeed we don't."

"Well, that's one thing I can clear up for you," Fairfax said. "The man wasn't connected with the case in any way at all. Actually, Mrs. Hoad was lunching with me."

"Really?" said Lawson. He contrived to look quite confused. "I *see*—I'm afraid that never occurred to us. . . . It looks as though we've been wasting our time, then. . . . Yours, too, I'm afraid. . . ." He picked up his hat—but his expression invited further information.

Fairfax said, in a faintly ironical tone, "If you're interested, it was Mr. Hoad's birthday the next day and Mrs. Hoad wanted to buy him something for his boat. She asked me to help her choose it, so I took her along to a yacht shop in the West End."

Lawson shot me a quick glance. A sceptical glance. I don't know what he'd have said next, but at that moment there was a ring at the door. Fairfax said, "Excuse me . . ." and went out into the passage and opened the door. Someone said, "Hallo, darling, am I late?" and a pretty, blonde girl appeared.

Fairfax said, "I've just been talking to the Press, Lena. About poor old John . . ." He introduced us. "Mr. Lawson! Mr. Curtis! My fiancée, gentlemen . . .! I'm sorry I can't help you further."

Chapter Nine

Lawson wasn't alone, of course, in thinking up farfetched theories. By now, almost everyone was doing it. Some of the theories were impersonal enough to be printed with safety. Some, like Lawson's, were highly defamatory and could only be discussed privately. Nothing was barred. One fairly fantastic suggestion was that the murderer had bribed a workman to make a cast of the key in cement, and had got into the castle that way. A variation was that the killer had got himself taken on as a workman and made his own key. Quite the wildest notion I heard was advanced by a man named Broadbent, who was covering the story for one of the mass-circulation picture papers. He had an idea that the castle key might have been stolen by Hoad himself. Broadbent's hypothesis was that Hoad the law-abiding citizen, the kind husband and father, was too good to be true; that he'd really been a very dark horse and had been concerned in some nefarious enterprise, possibly with a political flavour. The theory was that a gang had been using the castle as a safe nocturnal meeting place for four years, and that Hoad had been bumped off for some unknown reason by his former pals. But this was just the lunatic fringe of speculation.

Lawson, robbed of Fairfax, had reinstated Figgis as his chief suspect. He knew the police had grilled Figgis pretty thoroughly; he knew there was still no evidence that Figgis had ever met Hoad, and that his movements had been checked and that it was virtually established he hadn't left his house on the night of the murder. But Lawson had dreamed up a fresh possibility—that Figgis, though he hadn't committed the crime himself, had been in cahoots with the murderer and had lent him the castle key for the night. According to this new theory, Figgis's trip to London had been connected in some way with the making of the final arrangements. Lawson even went so far as to ask Blair to have inquiries made about Figgis's activities in London, and Smee spent a day on it, but he failed to discover any sinister contacts. The truth was that there wasn't an iota of real evidence against Figgis.

Soon, even the theories began to fizzle out. We were still without any new facts to base them on, and it began to look as though there weren't going to be any. No material clues had been discovered. No fingerprints had been found. No one had come forward with any evidence. Mrs. Hoad herself had been unable to throw any light on the tragedy. The police were daily becoming less communicative. There was an awkward vacuum; and presently rumours started to fly around. Cobley had made an arrest; he suspected a gipsy; he had discovered that a car had been parked by the kissing-gate on the night of the murder; he was going to drain the moat; he had found the weapon—and so on. Cobley patiently denied all the rumours, but he couldn't give us anything in their place. By the end of the fourth day, the story was beginning to look very tatty. Then we were suddenly told that the police had completed their inquiries in and around the castle and that Inspector Cobley was returning to his permanent H.Q. in the county town. That didn't mean, it was emphasised, that the case was being shelved—all it meant was that there was nothing more to be done around Lodden. But everyone behaved as though the story was over. Several reporters drifted away that evening. Figgis, bloody but unbowed, returned to London to resume his interrupted "course," and it was subsequently stated that the reopening of the castle would be postponed for a month to allow morbid public interest to die down. Lawson gathered together our last few scraps of information and phoned them—crediting them, as he always did, to "Curtis and Lawson." He explained the position to Blair, and Blair said we were both to return to the office in the morning. Personally, I felt quite ready to go. Mollie, I gathered, was staying on for a day or two, but only because she now had even more "days off" owing to her, not because she was expecting to pick up anything we'd missed. She said she was bored with the story—which actually had been apparent in her attitude for a couple of days. She had kept her end up adequately throughout the investigation, but this time she hadn't been anywhere near bringing off a spectacular coup. She hadn't even produced any very original theories. I pulled her leg about it a little, but she only laughed. "Even a star can't twinkle all the time," she said. I suggested that now that the work was done we should drive into Brighton and have dinner and perhaps dance, but she said she was tired. She didn't look tired. She never looked tired.

I sat up rather late that night, drinking bitter and talking shop with Lawson. By now he'd completely accepted me, and we got along fine together. He was fascinating about coroners' officers and post mortem indications and exhumations he'd attended, and it was nearly midnight when we went up to bed. Even then I wasn't in a hurry to turn in. The case had been disappointing, after the initial burst of excitement, but I felt stimulated and not at all in the mood for sleep. I sat in the window seat of my room, finishing my pipe, and gazing down at the quiet street.

The church clock struck twelve. As the last note died away I caught a sound from below which, at that time of night, was most unusual. It sounded like the front door of the pub being opened. I looked out, and saw a shadowy figure slip into the street and walk quickly away. It was Mollie!

I hesitated, but only for a second. It was just possible that she was simply in need of fresh air, but it seemed most unlikely. I remembered Lawson's advice—"Keep your eye on Mollie!" I crept downstairs and let myself out. I could still hear the light tap of her heels on the road. She was going up the hill towards the castle. I closed the door softly behind me and set off after her.

Chapter Ten

The night was very dark. Lodden's two street lamps were already out; not a light glimmered in any of the cottages. I groped my way up towards the kissing-gate. As long as I could feel the hard road under my feet, I was all right, but once I'd turned into the field I was lost and every step had to be taken with care. I couldn't imagine what Mollie thought she was up to. It wasn't as though these fields were without hazards in the dark. There was, I remembered, a deep ditch between the gate and the castle, crossed by a footbridge that one could easily miss. There was the moat itself. There was the river. And somewhere down on the right, running into the river, there was a small unfenced stream. A torch would have been very comforting.

I could see nothing of Mollie at all. I assumed that she must be making straight for the castle, and went cautiously forward in what I hoped was the right direction. As long as I kept going uphill I must come to the castle sooner or later. But when, after fifty yards or so, I stopped to listen, I thought I heard the sound of someone moving on my right, farther down the slope. Perhaps it was the river she was making for. I dropped down a little myself.

It was eerie, out there in the lonely darkness. Until now I'd taken a pretty impersonal view of the castle murder—I hadn't known or met any of the people directly affected, and to me it had been just a story, a mystery to be solved. To-night, I felt less detached. The battlements of the silent castle, which I could just make out now as a vague shape against the sky, had a brooding, sinister air. My mental picture of Hoad's face as his body had come gurgling up to the surface of the well was very vivid. The thought that a savage killer had been at work here so recently was unpleasant. Whatever it was that Mollie was up to, she had plenty of nerve. I couldn't hear her at all, now—she was obviously moving with the greatest care. For a while I stood still and listened—there seemed no point in going on when I didn't know where I was making for. I thought I heard faint stirrings in the grass around me. Maybe I was beginning to imagine things! Then a twig cracked sharply, away to the right. Mollie *was* down by the river. She seemed to be working her way round the foot of the castle hill. I felt quite baffled. If she'd had a torch it might have made some sense—but what on earth could she hope to discover in the dark?

I continued to stalk her. After each half-dozen steps, I stopped to listen again. I could hear her more clearly now—she appeared to have got mixed up with a hedge. Then, as the crackling died away, I heard another sound, and suddenly I felt my flesh creep. It was a slow, stealthy tread, and this time it came from *behind* me. There was some other person out here with us!

For a moment, I was frankly scared. The back of my head tingled as though a blunt instrument were already raised above it. If only I could *see* something! Then I took a grip on myself. If, for some reason, the murderer *had* returned to the scene of his crime, he was still only a man, and a man in the dark, like myself. I stood very still, listening. I could hear nothing now. I took ten paces downhill, and stopped once more. Again, for a second, I caught the sound of that cautious, menacing step—then, silence! Should I move towards him?—or should I wait? Waiting was unnerving. I took another step—and almost missed my footing. There seemed to be nothing in front of me but air. I crouched down and felt the ground with my hands and it fell away sharply. By now I had only the vaguest idea where I was. It couldn't be the moat, I was too far down the hill for that. Perhaps it was the river. With one hand outstretched, I lowered myself down the slope. After a moment I touched water. It was too shallow for the river—it must be the tributary. I drew back, listening. The movement behind me was louder. I heard the crunch of a stone. Whoever it was had flung caution away. This was it!—he was coming in for the kill! I braced myself. In the deep silence, I could even hear the grass being crushed. I could hear breathing, agitated breathing. A patch of sky grew darker than the rest as the shape of a man rose up above me. Well, attack was the best defence. I made a dive for him.

There was a fearful yell, and a moment of wild struggle, and then he went plunging down the bank into the stream. It was Lawson!

I couldn't see him, but judging by the gasping and splashing he was in a pretty panic. I called out in a fierce whisper, "It's me—Curtis! Come out, you clot!" There was a second's silence, and then he came clambering up the bank towards me, breathing hard. I stretched out a hand and helped him out. He was soaked from head to foot.

"God, old boy, you gave me a hell of a fright," he said.

"You gave me one, too. What on earth are you doing here?"

"Same as you, I suppose. I saw Mollie slip out and thought I'd better follow. I didn't realise you'd seen her, too. What's she up to?"

"I haven't a clue. I don't even know where she is, now."

He shivered. "Well, I'd better get back to the pub—I can't stick around in this state. What are you going to do?"

"I'll stay for a bit, now I'm here. Might as well check up on her. I'll be seeing you."

"Okay . . . Christ, I'm wet!" He turned and stumbled off into the darkness.

It had been a ridiculous episode, but at least it had broken the tension. Mollie must have heard us, so there was no point in keeping quiet any more. It was she who was keeping quiet, and I wasn't at all sure that I'd be able to find her. Still, I was much too curious to leave her without having a try. I worked my way cautiously down the bank of the stream and when I reached the river I turned left. It must have been about here, I decided, that Mollie had been in trouble with the hedge. Almost at once I reached the hedge myself. I found a way through, at the cost of minor scratches, and followed the river for fifty yards or so, stopping several times to listen. There wasn't a sound—I might have had the place to myself. Perhaps I had, I thought—perhaps Mollie had gone on along the river. In any case, it seemed unlikely that I should ever find her in this blackness. It was absurd—I'd be much better off in bed. I turned up the slope towards the castle. Near the top I stopped to listen again. As I did so, a voice almost at my feet said, "Is that you, Hugh?" I hadn't found Mollie—Mollie had found me.

I said "Yes" and felt my way towards her and dropped down beside her on the grass.

She said, "What's the idea of following me?"

"Magnetic attraction," I told her.

"Was that Lawson down there?"

"Yes. He's gone back to take a mustard bath." I told her what had happened.

"You are a couple of idiots."

"We had no choice. It's a rigid instruction at the *Record*—'Keep your eye on Mollie.' It's up on the notice board, signed by the Editor! What *are* you doing here, anyway?"

"Following a hunch."

"So I imagined. May I know what? I mean, if it comes off I'm bound to be in on it now, aren't I?"

"I don't suppose it will come off."

"Then you won't lose anything by telling."

"Well, it's quite simple. My idea is that Hoad may have been killed because he saw something he shouldn't have done."

"At the castle?"

"Probably."

"What would there have been to see in that empty shell?"

"I don't know, but someone might have been doing something there in secret."

"Like trying to demolish it for export, you mean?"

"You can jeer if you like, but it's about the only explanation that makes any real sense. As I see it, two men converged on this place who didn't know each other. One was Hoad, holiday-making, sight-seeing, curious. The other was a man who'd come back with a key after four years. And there was a collision."

"Well, it's an interesting thought," I said, "and you may be right.

But that still doesn't explain what you're doing here. The murderer's hardly likely to show up again."

"He might, if his work was interrupted."

"Wouldn't he have finished it before he left? After he'd tidied up the murder?"

"He wouldn't have had much time," Mollie said. "Getting rid of the body and scuttling the boat must have taken hours.... Anyway, if he'd thought he could finish it he'd hardly have gone to all that trouble to cover up what had happened. He'd simply have finished it and cleared off. At least, I should think so. I'd say he knew he had to come back."

"H'm! It's all guesswork, isn't it?"

"Of course. I told you—it's a hunch."

"Even if you're right, what makes you think he might turn up to-night?"

"It's the first night he could do it safely. The police have gone—the coast's clear."

"That's a point.... So how long do you plan to stay here?"

"Oh, an hour or two."

"I thought you said you were tired!"

She laughed softly.

"Well," I said, "what do you want me to do? Leave you to it?"

"I don't insist—not if you don't make a noise. Nobody's likely to come if we chatter."

"I won't make a sound," I said.

My eyes had got used to the darkness by now. I could make out the loom of the castle quite clearly. We were lying under a low bank about fifty yards from the moat. It was a good strategic spot. It was also a pleasant one. The grass was dry and fragrant. The air was balmy and full of summer scents. I lay back and relaxed. Mollie seemed pretty relaxed, too. She didn't give the impression that she expected anything much to happen—not as far as the castle was concerned, anyway. I wondered about other things. She was lying very close to me, and she didn't have to.

As the minutes passed, my thoughts moved farther and farther from the castle and concentrated more and more on Mollie. In broad daylight there had always been something faintly aloof about her, even when she was being friendly and charming; a "touch-me-not" something that had slightly scared me. Now, as she lay quietly beside me, I didn't have that feeling. I had quite different feelings. I moved my head a little, and tried to see her face. I could hear her quick breathing, I could just make out her features. She didn't move, and I kissed her mouth. I'd been wanting to do that ever since I'd set eyes on her. I'd doubted if I could get away with it, but it seemed I could. She still didn't move, not at first. She just let me kiss her, as though it were an interesting experiment. Then, suddenly, her arms went round me and she kissed me back with warmth and fervour. I hadn't expected that. There'd been nothing in her attitude to prepare me for fervour. I had an odd feeling that it couldn't really be meant for me; that maybe she wanted someone else very badly, only I happened to be around. Still, it was very pleasant—and very exciting. I began to hope we might really be going places—but as things began to warm up, she pushed me away.

"You take a long time to get to the starting point, Mr. Curtis," she said softly, "but there's nothing wrong with your acceleration. I think we'd better call it a night!"

It was then that the silence was broken by a peculiar grating sound. I think we'd both forgotten that we were supposed to be keeping watch, but now we were alert in a second. Someone had turned a key in the lock of the castle door!

Chapter Eleven

The thought did cross my mind at that moment that perhaps the most sensible thing would be to go and ring up the police—but then I'd only been a reporter for a week! Mollie didn't hesitate. "Come on," she said in a fierce whisper, "let's find out what's happening."

By the time I'd scrambled to my feet she was already up the bank. I joined her beside the moat, and with infinite caution we worked our way round the bank to the causeway. There was no risk of our being seen—noise was the only danger. We advanced on tiptoe to the door, which was shut. We stood tensely under the great portcullis, listening. All was quiet, inside and outside. Perhaps, I thought, we'd been mistaken about the grating noise. I grasped the iron ring that formed the handle, and began to turn it, very slowly and carefully. Even so, it squeaked a bit. When it was fully turned, I pushed against the door—and it moved. We hadn't been mistaken.

I put my shoulder to it and heaved gently, until there was a foot-wide gap. I stuck my head inside and peered round but there was absolutely nothing to be seen. The entrance passage with the "murder holes" over it was impenetrably dark. I slipped through the door, and Mollie followed. Somewhere, a night bird hooted, in the distance, the church clock struck two.

The courtyard seemed to be empty, but it was hard to tell. The uncertainty was spine-chilling. The man with the key might have heard us. He might be skulking in one of the alcoves, one of the hollow towers, anywhere. There were lots of places. If he was, we were almost bound to give ourselves away. Broken masonry lay across our path like a minefield. We were sure to make some noise. I thought of Hoad again, and what had happened to the back of his head—perhaps when he was doing just this thing. I stood there so long that Mollie grew impatient. "Get on!" she whispered. She was either less scared than I was, or less imaginative. I thought she was less scared.

I moved across the courtyard, with Mollie close behind me. I managed to avoid the obstructions but Mollie stumbled over something and for a moment we stood motionless, scarcely daring to breathe, listening. Nothing happened. The man with the key seemed to have melted away.

Then, somewhere ahead of us, high up, the silence was broken. There were three or four dull, heavy blows, as though someone was knocking in a tent peg with a wooden mallet. The sounds seemed to be coming from the square tower.

"Who said there were no noises in the night?" Mollie murmured in my ear.

We had reached the base of the tower now. The wooden door at the foot of the spiral staircase was closed. I eased it open gently. The sounds from above were more muffled inside, but I could still hear them. I began to climb the spiral, telling myself that as long as the noise went on I wasn't likely to meet anyone on the stairs. I stopped at the first-floor room and peered in, but it was empty. Mollie was pressing at my heels, and I continued to climb. As I rounded the last curve, I saw that the heavy wooden door giving on to the flat roof was standing open, and through it I caught the glimmer of a light. I sank down on the last step, beside the doorway, pressing myself against the wall so that Mollie could squeeze in beside me. Then, cautiously, we looked out.

There was an electric hand lamp on the roof, placed so that its light was focused on a section of the parapet. In the beam, a man was working. By now, I'd almost convinced myself that it would be Figgis, that it couldn't be anyone but Figgis—but it wasn't. This man was much bigger than Figgis. His face was turned away from us. He had a heavy hammer in his right hand, its head covered with a cloth to deaden the sound. In his left hand, he held something that looked like a chisel. He was breaking out the cement that the workmen had put into the parapet. A few feet to the right of him there was already a gaping hole, which he seemed to have abandoned. On the roof beside the lamp there was a soft travelling-bag and a coil of thick wire. This, beyond any doubt, was Hoad's murderer.

It wasn't easy to decide what to do. We were only a few feet from the man, and now I daren't even whisper to Mollie. We were terribly cramped. I was in the worst possible position to make a quick, silent approach and take him unawares. Once more, discretion suggested a quiet retreat for reinforcements. But Mollie might not want to go, and I couldn't leave her, and if we both went the man might get away. And I was desperately eager to know what he was up to. In the end, I did nothing.

We watched him for what seemed like an hour, though in fact it couldn't have been much more than twenty minutes. His blows on the chisel were strong and well-directed. Lumps of cement kept falling on the iron slats that guarded the overhang. The man obviously didn't mind how much mess he made—whatever he had begun, he meant to finish that night. He continued to hammer. Suddenly his chisel went through into a cavity like a dentist's probe, and he gave a little grunt of satisfaction and worked with redoubled energy to clear the debris. He pulled away several large lumps of cement, and put his hand in the hole and then his arm, and for a while he groped around inside. Then he picked up the coil of wire and cut a length off it with some pliers from his pocket, and bent one end into the shape of a hook. He pushed the wire into the hole and worked it along some sort of crevice to the left and began to fish around with it. Sweat glistened on his face. I still couldn't see his features properly. He poked and prodded and pulled for quite a while. Several times he drew the wire right out and bent the end into a different shape and started all over again. Either he couldn't hook the fish, or he couldn't land it, or there wasn't any fish there. He was certainly having extreme difficulty. Then, suddenly, a satisfied "Ah!" escaped him, and he withdrew the wire very slowly, very carefully, as though he had a trembler mine on the end of it. What, in fact, he had was something that looked like a wash-leather purse with a string that pulled tight at the neck. He dropped the wire and opened the neck of the purse and took out some small object which he held in his palm before the lamp. It flashed and sparkled, throwing out blue lights. After a moment he put it back and stuffed the purse into his pocket and began to collect up his tools. He was going to leave!

I'd been so fascinated watching him that I'd almost forgotten our own precarious position. Now we *had* to move. I put my mouth against Mollie's ear and whispered "*Back!*" She began to wriggle her body down, but we were tightly jammed on the narrow stairway and extrication wasn't easy. "*Hurry!*" I hissed. The man had zipped his bag shut and picked up the lamp. He was walking towards me. In a second he'd see me, and I'd be at his mercy. I knew then that we'd left it too late. There was only one thing to do. I struggled clear of Mollie and burst out of the doorway.

He was on to me like a panther, before I could even get upright. I caught one glimpse of a lean and ruthless face, and then I was flying across the roof. He came after me at once, but he'd had to drop the lamp and perhaps that fifth of a second saved me. I hit the parapet and scrambled away on all fours and grabbed wildly at a foot, which was all I could see of him. By a miracle I got hold of it and I jerked with all my strength. He fell with a crash and I grappled with him in the shadows. He was a powerful man, and there wasn't a nasty trick he didn't know. Happily he couldn't see what he was doing. I couldn't, either. For a few seconds we gouged and tore at each other on the concrete floor, rolling over and over. I landed a short-arm jab to his face that made him grunt, but a moment later he caught me an agonising blow in the groin with his elbow, and I fell back, writhing. He might have finished me then, but Mollie suddenly joined in, using the bag of tools like a two-handed axe, and though her blows weren't heavy they distracted him and gave me the respite I needed. I staggered to my feet and weaved around him, just out of reach, avoiding that murderous infighting of his, while the wave of pain passed. Then I went at him, punching with all my strength, and he punched back, and for a moment or two we slogged it out. I thought I had his measure now. I thought that with luck I could manage him. I ducked a haymaking left and caught him a cracking blow with my right on the side of the jaw, and he crashed back against the parapet and fell with a clang on the iron slats. It was an awkward fall, and he seemed to be in bad trouble. I rushed in to settle him, too recklessly, and he lashed out with his foot as he lay twisted on the ground and caught me sharply in the side. As I fell back his hand went to his pocket—and a moment later I was looking into the barrel of a gun.

"Back against the wall!" he said, breathing hard. "You too, girl!"

I hesitated, watching the gun. It didn't waver. His hand was steady. He was holding the gun like a man who was used to guns. I didn't think it was any stage property. I stepped back against the wall. Mollie moved across and joined me.

The man got slowly to his feet. One of his shoes, I noticed, had got caught up by the heel between the slats and had come off. For a second or two he studied us in silence. I could see his face quite clearly now. It was a surprising face for such a man—intelligent, good-looking, sardonic. But his eyes and mouth were utterly without pity. I thought he would make a most efficient executioner.

His finger tightened on the trigger, and he took half a step forward. Then he gave a little gasp, and stopped. He seemed concerned about his right foot, the one that had lost its shoe. Still covering us, he began to feel and rub it with his left hand. After a moment he made another attempt to put his weight on it, but he couldn't. His face wore a worried expression now. He stood there as though undecided what to do. Finally he hobbled round to the wooden door, using the parapet as a crutch, and pushed the door shut.

"Well, now," he said, "who *are* you?" He had an educated, almost a suave voice.

I told him who I was. I told him who Mollie was. It was the oddest introduction I'd ever made.

He nodded. "My name is Smith," he said. He was a man with a sense of humour! He asked if we were staying at the Castle Arms, and I said we were. He continued to study us in silence for a while. He still seemed to be debating what to do.

At last he said, "Well, this is all very awkward. As you can see, I've sprained an ankle rather badly. That's going to be very hampering for a man in my position. I'd planned to—well, to move about rather quickly. Now it looks as though I'll have to postpone my plans. In fact, it looks very much as though I'll have to rest up here for a day or two. Which means, of course, that I shall need your help—in quite a number of ways."

Neither of us said anything. There seemed nothing to say. He had the ball.

"We'll arrange things like this," he went on, after a moment. "You, Mr. Curtis, will be allowed to leave. You will get food, water and blankets, and to-morrow night you will come back here with them. In the meantime, Miss Bourne will stay here with me—as a hostage. You realise what that means, of course. If you give me away, if you attempt to bring anyone back with you, if the police come here—I shall kill her. To be precise, I shall shoot her in the stomach, and she will die in agony. . . . Did you ever see anyone die that way?"

"You must be mad," Mollie said.

"Not mad, Miss Bourne—just desperate. Unless I can get clear away I'm a man with absolutely nothing to lose. As you undoubtedly realise, I killed Hoad. If I'm caught, I shall have to pay the penalty for that. If I kill you, too, I shall still only have to pay the same penalty. Two for the price of one, you might say—and no extra charge for the method used! So why should I hesitate?"

Off-hand, I couldn't think of any reason why he should.

"At the same time," he said, "if you co-operate with me loyally for a day or two, you need have nothing to fear. When I can move about again comfortably, which should be in about three days' time, I shall leave here and let you both go free. I've no desire to kill either of you—particularly such a charming young lady as yourself, Miss Bourne. Before you can put anyone on my trail, I shall be out of reach. So you see, I can afford to offer you your lives—as a prize for good behaviour. Our interests are really identical—we all want to get away safely, and there's no reason why we all shouldn't. Well, Mr. Curtis, what do you say?"

"The police may come anyway," I said. "The caretaker may come. Anyone may come. The odds are hopelessly against you."

"If anyone comes, I shall have to start shooting—and I'm afraid Miss Bourne may be the first victim. But why should they? The police have finished their work here. Figgis is in London until the end of the week. The castle is always kept locked. No one will come—except you."

Mollie said, "They may come and look for me. They're bound to start searching if I don't go back to the hotel."

"That's something we must take care of, Miss Bourne. You must write a note to the manager—I'm sure you have paper and a pencil with you. Make it sound as though it was written very early to-morrow morning—as though you'd suddenly decided to go off for a day or two but were leaving most of your things and wanted your room kept. Mr. Curtis will see that it's delivered."

"If it was written in the morning," Mollie said, "my bed would have been slept in. And it won't have been."

"Ah . . .!" Smith considered that for a moment, "Is your room locked?"

"No."

"Then Mr. Curtis can attend to the bed when he goes back to-night."

"My car's parked at the hotel—I'd never go away for two or three days without that."

"Then Mr. Curtis must look after the car, too. I expect a little initiative. After all, it's your own lives that are at stake." The gun jerked. "Please—the note!"

Mollie looked at me—and gave a helpless shrug. She took a pad from her bag, and wrote.

When she'd finished, Smith said, "Give your car ignition key to Mr. Curtis."

She gave it to me.

"Now put the pad in your bag and throw the bag across to me. Gently!"

She tossed it at his feet. He put the gun on top of the parapet and opened the bag and took the note out. He held it so that the light fell on it, and began to read it with every sign of concentration. He was about four yards away from me. I thought I could just make it. I raised myself on my toes and sprang towards him. But before I was half-way there he'd whipped up the gun and had me covered again.

"You have a strange idea of co-operation, Mr. Curtis," he said quietly. "That was very foolish, you know—I'm hardly a child in these matters. Get back to the wall. I'll deal with you in a moment."

I stepped back, beaten, and re-joined Mollie. She said, "Don't try it, Hugh—it's too risky." Smith said, "That's right, Miss Bourne—use your influence." He finished reading the note, put it back in the bag, and threw the bag back to Mollie. "Yes, that's all right," he said. "The handwriting's a little shaky, perhaps, but I expect it will pass. Give the note to Mr. Curtis."

She gave it to me and I put it in my pocket.

There was a little silence. Then Smith said, "It seems, Mr. Curtis, that you still don't quite realise what sort of man I am. Obviously you need a lesson—just to teach you not to do these rash things. Just to teach you what desperation means. Stand away from Miss Bourne!"

I moved six feet along the parapet. He waved me still farther along. Then he began to hobble painfully round the roof towards me. He still had me covered. His face was quite impassive—he looked more like an executioner than ever. As he drew nearer, I braced myself for a blow.

But it didn't come. Instead, he stepped up close to Mollie and pressed the gun into her stomach. "I'm going to hit Miss Bourne," he said. "If you make a move, Mr. Curtis, I shall shoot her." He struck her hard across the face with his left hand. Involuntarily I started forward, but Mollie's warning cry and the wicked little gun checked me.

"You can't argue with a gun, you know," Smith said softly. "You can't be chivalrous in face of a gun. You could try, of course, but it would go off before you could do any good. And as far as Miss

Bourne is concerned, it would precipitate the very thing you want to avoid. In face of a gun, you have to learn self-control. You have to learn to accept the lesser evil."

He slapped her face again.

"You see what I mean?" he said. "If you hadn't kept a tight hold on yourself then, Mr. Curtis, she'd be dead. You'd have forced me to kill her. And, of course, you too. What good would that have done to anyone? Your only hope is to co-operate."

He stretched out his hand and gripped the neck of Mollie's blouse and with one fierce wrench he tore her clothes open to the waist.

"Well, Mr. Curtis?" he said.

Sweat poured into my eyes. I said, in a shaking voice, "Be careful . . .!"

"Of course I shall be careful. Everyone has his breaking point, and I don't doubt that you could be provoked into rash intervention. But then, you see, I've stopped short of the breaking point. . . . Well, now that you've had your lesson, you'd better be on your way."

I looked at Mollie. She was trying to hold her torn clothing together, not very successfully. She looked terribly pale in the wan electric light. She said, "You'd better go, Hugh. We've no choice."

"But I can't leave you with him."

"You must. I'll be all right. It's the only way."

I turned savagely to Smith. "All right," I said. "But if Miss Bourne comes to any harm while she's with you, I swear I'll get you if I have to follow you to the ends of the earth." It was a stupid cliché of a threat—but it was what I felt.

"A nice speech," he said. "Very creditable sentiments. I'll bear it in mind."

He produced a big key from his pocket. "The key to the castle," he said. "The *spare* key! You'll need it. Don't forget to lock up behind you when you leave—we don't want anyone wandering in through an open door. . . . Now let me see. . . . You might try to get hold of some sort of bandage for my ankle when you do your shopping—it's in the interests of all of us that it should get better quickly. And bring us something nice to eat—I suggest a little cold chicken. But you probably know Miss Bourne's tastes. Some wine wouldn't come amiss—and glasses, of course. We'd like to be as civilised as we can while we're camping out. But I'll leave all the details to you. Come as soon as you can after dark—I'm sure Miss Bourne will get very hungry and thirsty. And don't try any foolish tricks like putting cyanide in the sandwiches—I've my official taster here. Good night, Mr. Curtis."

I moved towards the door, and opened it.

"Watch your step," he said. "Watch it all the way. You've a valuable life in your charge, so be careful."

I said, "All right, Mollie?"

She nodded. She had herself well under control. "All right, Hugh. This is going to make quite a story in the end."

I turned and descended the steps. There didn't seem anything else to do.

Chapter Twelve

I crossed the courtyard in a kind of daze. I locked the castle door behind me mechanically. I walked down the field path in revolt against the facts. The whole affair was too gangsterish, too utterly melodramatic to be credible. This sort of thing, I told myself, just didn't happen in England. It was going to take a lot of getting used to.

I felt ghastly. Not physically, though I had plenty of bruises and aches. Mentally. I'd behaved like a damned fool. It had been crazy to go spying on a murderer virtually single-handed. It had been crazy to get wedged on those stairs. I'd certainly asked for trouble. And then I'd bungled the fight. I ought to have thought about a gun while there was still time. I oughn't to have given Smith a chance to pull it on me. . . . Worst of all, I'd stood by and watched Mollie being savagely ill-treated. It was no good telling myself that if I hadn't she'd have been dead by now. I felt a louse.

There was only one consolation—and I didn't know how long it would remain one. If I hadn't followed Mollie to the castle, if she'd stumbled alone upon the man, he'd almost certainly have killed her out of hand.

I was still pretty dazed when I reached the hotel. I still hadn't come to terms with the situation. I still couldn't quite believe it. But I knew I'd got to act as though I did. I slipped into the lobby and turned the key behind me and stole silently upstairs. My room came first, then Lawson's, then Mollie's. There was only a feeble light in the corridor, and outside Lawson's door I stumbled over his shoes. They made a hell of a clatter, but no one stirred. I opened Mollie's door and went in and closed it behind me. The curtains were already drawn across the window, and I switched on the light. At that dead hour of the morning the switch made a frightful row, too, but I had to have a light. There was a fragrance in the room that took me straight back to Mollie, and I felt worse than ever. Heaven alone knew what sort of a sadist Smith might be—and she was utterly in his power. But I couldn't help her, and I put the thought out of my mind and concentrated on the job. I had to make the scene convincing. I loosened the pillows, and made a dent in one of them with my fist, and mussed up the bedclothes. I damped one of the towels and threw it carelessly over the towel rail. I moistened the soap. I put a little tooth-paste in one of the tumblers and swilled it around with some water. Then I gathered up a few things that Mollie would certainly have taken with her—her nylon nightie from the bed, a thin silk dressing-gown from the wardrobe, her hairbrush and toothbrush and a few other toilet things from the shelf above the basin and from the dressing-table. I stuffed the nightie and the smaller things into my pockets, and the dressing-gown inside my jacket, and took a last look round. The state of the room might not have deceived a detective but it looked all right to me and I thought it would to a chamber-maid. I switched off the light, cautiously drew the curtains, opened the door, and crept out.

As I did so, another switch clicked on and Lawson's door opened, sending a flood of light into the corridor. He peered out just in time to catch me in the act of leaving. For a moment he gazed at me as though he couldn't believe his eyes. Then his pale face split in a fatuous grin.

"Oh, naughty, naughty!" he said, under his breath, and tut-tutted.

"What the hell are you snooping about for?" I burst out, in an angry whisper.

"Sorry, old boy, I'm a light sleeper. Don't worry, I'll keep mum. You lucky chap!" He gave an awful leer. "Anything happen out there by the castle?"

"Not a thing!"

He grinned again. "Okay, see you in the morning," he said, and went back into his room.

At least, I thought, I'd established Mollie's presence in the hotel to Lawson's satisfaction!

I walked past his door and into my own room and stuffed Mollie's things into the bottom of my suitcase. I looked at my watch and saw that it was half past three. Very soon, it would be daylight. Any thought of sleep was out of the question. I drank a pint of water and bathed my bruised face. Then I sank down on the window seat and tried to get things straight in my mind. I knew I had to do something, but I hadn't the slightest idea what.

The natural thing was to enlist help—but I didn't see how I could. I tried to imagine what the police would do if I did bring them into it, how they would set about coping—and I couldn't think of anything that wouldn't put Mollie in mortal danger. There was no way in which they could safely tackle Smith in his tower stronghold. There was no way I could take him by surprise. I mentally canvassed the wildest possibilities, from tear gas to lowering someone from a helicopter, but there was always one insuperable snag. Smith would be able to shoot Mollie before any attack could be pressed home. He could act at the first sign, the first sound. What was more, I hadn't the slightest doubt that he would do so. I'd have liked to believe he was bluffing, but I couldn't. If, by my action, he was driven into a corner, he'd shoot—just to square the account. Even if I was wrong, I couldn't take the risk. So the police were out.

If, on the other hand, I kept quiet and carried out my instructions, both Mollie and I ought to be safe enough for the time being. Smith's position, I now saw, wasn't quite as strong as I'd supposed during the stress of the castle encounter. On the broad issue, he had the whip hand—I couldn't give him away. But as long as I didn't give him away, and he was still confined to the castle on account of his crippled foot, he'd need me around in good working order, because he'd need supplies. If he was stuck in the castle for several days without food and water he'd be in pretty poor shape for making a getaway at the end of it—and he knew that. And he couldn't just order me to bring supplies for all the time he was likely to be there, and then dispose of us. For one thing, he didn't know yet how long he was going to be there. For another, if *I* disappeared without trace there'd be no one to cover up for me at the hotel. And he certainly wouldn't want any more mysteries in Lodden until he was safely out of reach. He'd been quick enough to take the point over Mollie. It seemed, therefore, that I could rely on being free, with Mollie cherished as a hostage, until the moment came for his departure.

But what then? When I considered the position from his point of view, I simply couldn't believe that he'd let us go in the end. We didn't know everything about him, but we knew far too much. We knew that he was probably a jewel thief, and in a pretty big way of business. We could describe him in detail. If he already had a criminal record, which seemed quite likely, the police would be able to identify him at once. In any case, his description would be circulated everywhere, on the Continent as well as in England, and the chances were high that he'd be picked up. But if he could leave the castle secretly, as he'd come, without anyone knowing anything about him or his visit, he'd be safe, because there'd be no one on his trail. So, once again, why should he hesitate? He'd do to us what he'd done to Hoad—he'd silence us. We should end up in the well or the moat. It was as certain as a Euclidean proof.

The conclusions from all this were only too clear. First, if anyone was going to get us out of this mess, it would have to be me. The burden of responsibility sat squarely on me; I was the only person who could hope to make an opportunity. And since, if I failed, there was no future for us anyway, I'd have to be prepared to take pretty desperate risks, even fantastic risks. Nothing, however bizarre, could be ruled out.

Sitting there on the window seat, with another lovely dawn just beginning to break, I considered every way I could think of to catch Smith unawares. I thought of trying to get hold of a gun myself and taking a pot at him when he opened the door to the roof. I'd used a revolver a bit in the Army—I knew the butt from the barrel. Still, I'd never been much of a shot with it; and Smith had handled his gun with the speed of a cowboy in a Western. I didn't give much for my chances in a gun duel. He'd probably be expecting something like that, too. He'd be pretty sure to be on his guard. Anyone would, in his position.

I thought of trying to conceal some weapon among the food supplies. It might be worth an attempt—though I hadn't much doubt that he'd notice it. He hadn't missed a trick so far, and from what I'd seen of him I didn't think he'd ever miss anything as obvious as that.

I thought of trying to get hold of a rifle, and picking him off from the shelter of the hazel bushes beside the moat. It seemed unlikely that he'd expose himself much on the battlements in daylight, but he might in the very early morning. Or he might show up at one of the loopholes. The trouble was that if I failed to get him with my first shot I shouldn't have another chance—and he'd almost certainly regard the attempt as a declaration of war, which could well be the end of Mollie. That was no good, either. Not at this stage, anyway.

Perhaps I could draw him out of the tower by some ruse?—create some diversion, manoeuvre him into a position of disadvantage? That was fine in theory, but specifically I couldn't think how. Perhaps I could manage something while he was asleep—he'd obviously have to sleep sometime. I wondered what sort of dispositions he was making at the castle. How, for instance, would he ensure that Mollie herself didn't get troublesome while he was sleeping? I really needed to know a good deal more before I could make any plans.

Meanwhile, a minor problem was what I was going to do about Lawson and the office. Clearly I'd have to think up some good reason why I couldn't go back—something that wouldn't rouse any suspicion or start any inquiry. The last thing I wanted was that Lawson should get suspicious. Illness!—that was the thing. I'd have to say I wasn't well. No one ever argued about that.

By now it was five o'clock, and full daylight, and I concentrated again on the immediate tasks. I had to move Mollie's car before the hotel servants were up. I also had to leave her message somewhere, I crept downstairs to the lounge and got a hotel envelope from a drawer and slipped the note inside it. The window of the reception desk was closed, but a heavy inkwell had been left on the ledge outside and I put the envelope underneath it. It probably wouldn't be noticed till around eight, by which time Mollie could easily have left. So far, so good! I crossed to the front door and unlocked it and went out into the street. It was a beautiful morning again—the sort of morning that made you feel you wanted to live for ever. I walked round the back of the hotel to the car park. Mollie's car was parked against a wall and it wasn't visible from any of the windows, even if anyone had been looking. I squeezed myself into the driving-seat and started the engine and drove quietly away. I'd noticed a biggish garage in Worley when I'd been over there to see the inspector, and I drove straight to it and stopped outside. Then I settled down for a long wait. A milkman came by soon after six, and a postman just before seven, and then the place began to get quite busy—but no one gave me more than a passing glance. At ten minutes past eight a man arrived to open the garage. I asked him if I could leave my car there for a few days and he said, "Certainly, sir!" and gave me a ticket. He didn't appear to think there was anything odd about my parking a car at that hour in a place like Worley. I walked to the nearest bus stop and looked at the timetable and there was a bus back to Lodden in fifteen minutes. It got me to the pub just before nine. Mollie's message, I saw, had gone from the reception desk. I nodded a "Good morning!" to the manager's wife and went into the dining-room. I felt extremely hungry, but I daren't order much of a breakfast—if I was going to malinger, it wouldn't do to let Lawson catch me wolfing bacon and eggs. I asked for coffee and a roll, and thought of Mollie sitting up there in the tower all day without food or water. I hadn't much to complain of.

I'd just finished my second cup when Lawson came in. He looked very chipper. He said, "Oh, what a beautiful morning!" and sat down opposite me. He picked up the menu and gave me a sly glance. Then his jaw dropped.

"Christ, old boy," he said, "what have you been doing to your face?"

I'd forgotten he hadn't seen my bruises in daylight. Not that they were all that bad, now, but they were something. I said, "My wardrobe door was open and I walked into it in the dark. I'm surprised you didn't hear me."

He grinned. "Sure it wasn't Mollie trying to save her honour?"

"It was not," I said shortly.

"Well, you certainly don't look so good. How do you feel?"

"Lousy," I said. "Very tired."

"What do you expect, old boy . . .? By the way, what *was* Mollie up to at the castle?"

"I don't think she was up to anything. She just said she couldn't sleep."

"That's a likely story! Where did you run into her?"

"Outside the pub, as a matter of fact. I caught her up at the door on my way back."

"Nice timing! Is she around yet?"

"She was—but she went off early. Said something about going to stay with friends for a day or two."

"You mean she's checked out?"

"No, I gather she's left some of her things. She said she just couldn't be bothered to pack."

"Bit odd, isn't it?"

"She's an odd girl," I said vaguely.

"You should know, old boy!"

He didn't pursue the subject. I saw him talking to the manager a bit later, but it didn't get him anywhere. I had a word with the manager myself and pulled his leg about having nothing to do now that most of the newspapermen had left and said I understood Miss Bourne had gone off early, and he nodded. He seemed quite unconcerned. By now, reporters were probably all crazy to him, anyway.

Around ten-thirty, Lawson said that we might as well be getting on our way. I was just going to tell him I didn't feel up to it when there was a call from the office, and he took it. He talked for a minute or two, and then called out that Blair wanted me and handed the receiver over.

Blair said briskly, "Oh, Curtis, I'd like you to get back here as quickly as you can. There's a good story for you up in Norfolk."

I said, "I'm sorry, Mr. Blair, but I'm afraid I'm not well."

"Not well? Why, what's the matter, Curtis?"

"Sickness," I said. "Frightful headache. . . ." I suddenly realised that I was making it sound far too much like a hangover and added quickly, "Bit of fever, too. I think I've caught a chill. I honestly don't feel fit for work."

"Well, it's very inconvenient," he said in a testy voice. "We're extremely short-handed here."

"I'm sorry," I said again.

He grunted. "If you're ill, you're ill, I suppose. Anyway, see how you get on. Give me a call this afternoon."

"Very well," I said—and rang off. That hurdle seemed to have been taken all right.

Lawson was just putting his bag into his car. I felt an immense relief. "You're off, are you?" I said.

"Yes—smash-and-grab at Aldershot. What about you?"

"I've had to duck my job," I said. "I'm simply not feeling up to it."

"Really?" Lawson looked quite shocked. "I'm afraid you lack stamina, old boy."

I smiled feebly at him. "I blame the wardrobe."

"What are you going to do? Go home?"

"No, I think I'd better stick around here for a while and take it easy."

He gave a faint shrug. He obviously thought I was miking, and took a poor view, but I couldn't have cared less. "Well, I'll be seeing you," he said. He got into his car, and a moment later he was driving away. I'd never been happier to see the back of anyone. He was the last of the reporters to leave. I took a deep breath, and began to consider the next problem.

Chapter Thirteen

If only for Mollie's sake, I'd obviously got to make an efficient job of laying in supplies. She would need at least two blankets—even with the mild nights we were having it must be pretty chilly in that bare stone castle—and that meant two for Smith as well. I should have to buy some sort of container for water, and there was Smith's bandage to get, and I should need quite a bit of food. Brighton, I decided, was the best place to shop—I'd be lost in the crowd there and no one would give a second thought to my rather unusual purchases. I drove in shortly after twelve and parked the Riley and had lunch. Then, as soon as the shops opened again, I started on my rounds. I bought a two-gallon can for water at an ironmonger's, and some grey blankets from a large store. I got an elasticised bandage from a chemist's. I bought two tumblers and a collection of assorted cutlery. I didn't suppose they'd actually need knives and forks, but it seemed the most promising way of getting potentially dangerous weapons into the castle. One of the knives, in particular, was short and strong and very sharp. I also bought a corkscrew and a pretty lethal tin opener. I picked up some milk and a loaf, and then went into a provision store for the main supplies. I'd scribbled out a shopping-list in the car. As I stood at the counter, watching cooked ham being sliced up, the fantastic unreality of the whole business came over me again. It seemed absolutely incredible that I was buying groceries for a murderer—that I was proposing to take them along to him, tamely, as though I were some sort of delivery boy. But I still didn't see what else I could do . . .

The man behind the counter said, "Anything more, sir?"

I looked at the pile of things—ham and tongue, tinned meat, butter, cheese, chocolate, biscuits, tomatoes, fruit. The prisoners in the tower certainly wouldn't starve now—and what with the blankets and the water I doubted if I should be able to carry much more. I glanced around the shelves to see if there was anything I'd overlooked—and my eyes came to rest on a small round tin. It was labelled "White Pepper."

Pepper!

It was an old idea, of course, as old as the hills—but that seemed all the more reason why it might work. It was certainly the best idea I'd had yet. I said I'd have it.

I took the groceries back to the car and sat there for a while, thinking about the pepper. If I put it in with the rest of the supplies, I couldn't see that I'd have any chance of using it. For one thing, the tin was sealed, and it might remain sealed. Smith might not like pepper. If I opened it myself, it probably wouldn't pass his vigilant eye. Perhaps it would be better if I put some of it in a screw of paper and tried to smuggle it in in my pocket. He could easily miss that. But taking it out and unfolding it without being noticed and using it on him when he was within striking distance wouldn't be very simple. Throwing pepper probably wouldn't be very simple, anyway. What I needed was some little gadget that would direct a jet of it straight at him. But how and where would I hide it?

I thought about it for some time, and presently I had a new idea. I went back to the shops and began to look around for an insufflator. I'd never realised before how many different types there were on the market. There were sprays of every size and description—glass ones and plastic ones and metal ones, sprays with long nozzles and large rubber bulbs, sprays with small nozzles and scarcely any bulbs at all. In the end, I found just what I wanted on a cosmetic counter. It was a small pink container of some soft, collapsible material, with a very short black plastic nozzle set at a slight angle. I could scarcely wait to try it.

I walked quickly back to the car, and opened the pepper tin, and poured a little pepper into the container. Then I screwed up the nozzle, and opened my jacket and put the nozzle through the top buttonhole from the inside and buttoned up. I got out of the car and walked about a bit to see if it was secure and the thing seemed to be held quite firmly by the nozzle, which was pointing slightly upwards and away from me. I made sure no one was watching, and gave the top of my jacket a smart tap, and a fine spray of pepper shot out for more than a foot. Some of it drifted back on me, and I was seized with a paroxysm of sneezing and for a moment or two my eyes streamed. It seemed to work very well! If only I could direct the spray into Smith's face, I hadn't a doubt that he'd be temporarily incapacitated. A mere second off guard would be enough for me to get his gun. And in the half-light of the castle roof, I didn't think he'd notice the nozzle. It protruded scarcely half an inch. Anyhow, it was worth trying.

I put the insufflator away and drove back to the Castle Arms. I filled the water can from the hose pipe in the car park, and left the stores locked up in the car in a soft bag. It was now nearly four o'clock and I decided I must try to get a little sleep. It wouldn't help anyone if I reached the castle in an exhausted state. I went up to my room and stretched out on the bed. The next thing I knew, it was six o'clock, and a maid was tapping on my door and saying there was a telephone call for me.

I'd forgotten all about the office. I'd forgotten I'd been told to ring Blair. I hurried down to the box and picked up the receiver. It wasn't Blair, it was Hatcher, and he was in his nastiest mood.

"I thought you were supposed to be ill!" he said.

"I am."

"We tried to get you after lunch and they said you'd gone out. Bloody strange illness!"

"I wanted to get some fresh air," I said,

"Well, there's plenty of fresh air in Norfolk—you'd better come back."

"I'm really not fit," I said.

"Have you seen a doctor?"

"Well, no . . ."

"Then see one."

"It's just an indisposition," I said. "I'll be all right in a day or two."

He blew his top, then—and I couldn't blame him. "A day or two! That's no bloody good. We run a newspaper here, not a bloody convalescent home. I don't believe there's anything wrong with you at all. See a doctor right away and let me know what he says. That's an order!"

He hung up.

I felt pretty worried. If I didn't report, they'd be sure to ring again the next day. And they'd keep on ringing. If I continued to stall, they'd probably send someone down to find out what the hell I was playing at. They might even send Lawson back, which was the very last thing I wanted. It was absolutely imperative that I should be left alone for the next few days. I thought about it for a long time, and there seemed only one thing to do. I went into the lounge and composed a letter to Blair. It took me quite a while. The final version read:

DEAR MR. BLAIR,

I'm afraid that I must ask you to accept, as of now, my resignation from the post of reporter on the *Record*. I have been reluctant to take this step, particularly in view of the consideration that you and other members of the staff have shown me, but I realise now that I am temperamentally unfitted for the life. As you may have guessed, there is nothing really wrong with my health, but this ghastly murder has upset my nerves and I'm not sleeping at all well. I find that I dislike intensely the sort of inquiries that reporters have to make, and I can't at all approve of some of the methods they use. In the circumstances, it is obviously better that I should find some other sort of work, so please accept this as a final severance. If there should be any letters for me, I'd be grateful if you would have them redirected to me at Poste Restante, General Post Office, Launceston, as I am proposing to take a holiday in Cornwall right away before looking around for a new job.

Yours sincerely,

HUGH CURTIS

I sealed the letter up and drove into Brighton to post it so that Blair would be sure to get it first thing in the morning. I hadn't much doubt that it would do the trick. Blair didn't know me at all well—he would take it at its face value and write me off as a hopeless neurotic and hypochondriac. There might be repercussions later on, because I'd been taken on to the staff of the *Record* very much as a favour, and the Chairman was pretty certain to mention what had happened, to my father. But he couldn't do it at the moment because my father was away in Lausanne at a conference until the middle of June. By then, if I came through this business, I'd be able to explain everything. If I didn't come through, it would scarcely matter. I felt much happier when the letter was posted.

The rest of the evening dragged horribly. I went to my room around ten and waited there in a state of mounting tension, listening to the quarters striking. I couldn't leave the hotel until the manager had locked up and gone to bed, because otherwise I should be locked out. Anyway, it would be safer to wait until the village was asleep. From my window seat, I watched the lights go out one by one. When all seemed quiet, I crept downstairs and silently let myself out. It was five minutes to midnight. I'd already taken the precaution of parking the car beside the kissing-gate, and I walked quickly up the hill to it. There was no one about. I took the blankets under one arm, and the water can and soft bag with all the provisions in it in the other, and set off up the field path. I had to walk very slowly and carefully, because the insufflator was in position and I didn't want to set it off with any sudden jerk and arrive at the castle sneezing and smelling of pepper!

The night was almost as dark as the previous one had been, but I was getting to know the place better now and I had little difficulty in finding my way. I skirted the moat, passed below the square tower, and crossed the causeway to the door. I rested for a moment, for I was carrying quite a load. Then I let myself in with Smith's key. I tried to lock the door again behind me, but I found that I couldn't. Apparently there was some obstruction in the lock, so that it worked from the outside but not from the inside. That cleared up a point which had puzzled me quite a bit—why Smith had left the door open behind him on the night when Hoad had walked in on him. Evidently he'd had no choice.

I crossed the courtyard to the tower door, and pulled it open, and called up softly. I thought that Smith and Mollie might be in the first-floor room, but I got no reply. I lugged the bag up the spiral staircase and reached the top door, which was closed. I couldn't see a thing. I made sure the insufflator was still in position, and banged on the door. There was a moment's silence. Then Smith called out, "Is that you, Mr. Curtis?"

"Yes," I said.

"Have you got the stuff?"

"Yes." I was so tense with excitement that it was all I could do to keep my voice under control. "There's a bit more to come up."

"Fetch it, then."

I left the bag on the step and went down for the blankets and water. As I reached the top door again I put my shoulder to it and heaved, just to see what would happen. It gave a little, but it didn't open. It felt as though Smith had his foot wedged against it. He called out, "Easy, there!" I waited. After a moment the door opened about six inches. A pale gleam of light came through from the roof. I couldn't see Mollie.

Smith said, "Put both your hands through the door, Mr. Curtis. And keep them there."

I obeyed. The door slowly opened. The first thing I saw was the gun, well out of reach. The next thing was Smith. He certainly wasn't taking any chances. I hadn't overestimated him.

"Step in," he said. "Hands above your head. Now stand still." He hobbled up close. I could see that he still wasn't putting much weight on his foot. He thrust the gun against my belly and slapped my pockets expertly. Out of the corner of my eye I could just see the nozzle of the insufflator—though only because I knew it was there. It was pointing straight at his face, and I knew it would work if only I could get at it. He thumped my breast pocket and must have been within an inch or two of triggering it off himself—but he missed it. "All right," he said, and stepped back. I lowered my hands, sweating with disappointment. The moment had passed.

I looked around for Mollie. She was sitting propped up in an angle of the parapet, with her thin summer coat folded under her as a cushion. I said, "Hallo, Mollie. Are you all right?"

"More or less," she said. She sounded as though she was having difficulty with her voice, too—but with her it wasn't excitement. I guessed it was just plain misery. "I could do with a drink—I'm absolutely parched."

"I'll get it," Smith said. He backed to the door, and brought in the bag and the water can. He opened the bag as carefully as though it had been full of grenades. He took the things out one at a time, and scrutinised each in turn.

"What goes with this?" he asked, holding up the corkscrew.

"I couldn't get any wine," I said. "I left it too late and the hours were wrong. I'll bring some to-morrow."

He grunted, and went on delving. He spread everything neatly on the concrete—the tumblers, the tins, the knives and forks, the packets of this and that. He had a delicate touch with everything, like a conjurer or a card sharper. He never fumbled. When he came to the dagger-like knife he gave me a quick, sardonic glance, tried the point, and tossed it over the parapet into the moat. But he passed the tin opener. He inspected the bandage, and seemed to approve of it.

"Well, that seems all right," he said, surveying the things. "You've been busy, Mr. Curtis." He unscrewed the top of the water can, smelt the contents, and filled the two tumblers. He took one over to Mollie, and himself drained the other at a draught. He refilled them, and they both drank again. They certainly were thirsty. Then he fetched the blankets, unrolled them carefully, and put two of them beside Mollie and two beside his jacket, which lay across the slats behind the door. It seemed that I'd been right about the door—he'd obviously been sitting there with his foot against it. That way, of course, he couldn't be taken by surprise. He pushed the door shut, now, and set to work to carve up a loaf. The gun was on the concrete beside him, but I wasn't tempted. Not at the moment. I was still hoping for a chance to use the pepper.

I walked over to Mollie. So far she hadn't moved. The light from the handlamp was dimmer than the night before and I still couldn't see her face properly. I said, "Has he behaved himself?"

"So far," she said.

"Have you been up here all the time?"

"No, only since dusk. We spent most of the day in the courtyard. I'm allowed to exercise!"

"Are you going to sleep up here?"

"I gather so. Mr. Smith has fixed up a gadget so that I can't cut his throat during the night."

She pointed, and I saw then that one of her feet was secured by wire to the slats. There were two separate wires, and two separate loops. The whole thing was cunningly arranged so that she couldn't get free unaided. The ends of the wires were both out of her reach.

I said indignantly, "Look here, Smith, you can't leave her like this!" Even as I said it, it struck me that indignation was pretty foolish in the circumstances. It was like complaining of discomfort on the way to the gas chamber. But that was how it was. One became almost conditioned to major outrage, and boggled over detail.

Smith was quite unperturbed. He was dividing ham and tongue and tomatoes into two heaps with meticulous care. He said, "She's perfectly all right, Mr. Curtis—the wires aren't tight. Obviously I can't leave her free at night. Even if she didn't cut my throat, she might get desperate and jump into the moat. I wouldn't like her to hurt herself!" He picked up his gun, and half the food. "Just stand away, will you, while I bring this over?"

I stood back, and he took the food across to Mollie. Then he returned to his place, and they both began to eat. They were both ravenous. While they ate, I gave Mollie the news. I told her about Lawson and the bedroom incident, because I thought it might cheer her up a bit, and it did. I also told her where I'd put her car, and about my office ringing up, and about the letter of resignation I'd sent to Blair. She seemed quite horrified over that, but she had to agree that it had been the only thing to do. Smith grunted approval. He seemed very amiable. He didn't mind Mollie and me talking. He didn't seem to mind anything. Actually, it wasn't easy to talk, because I had half my mind on how I could get near enough to him to use the pepper.

As I gazed around at the uniquely improbable scene, I had to tell myself all over again that this wasn't just a nightmare. For it really was fantastic. There, in one corner, was Mollie—the haughty, sophisticated Mollie—tethered by a foot like some animal. There, in another corner, was Smith, a callous and apparently quite unworried murderer, thoroughly enjoying his food and behaving as politely as a host at a party. And there was I, with a woman's powder spray sticking out of my buttonhole, and homicide in my heart. And all in the sinister, shadow-casting half-light of that now failing electric lamp. It seemed incredibly macabre.

At last Smith stirred. "Well, that was good," he said. "To-morrow, Mr. Curtis, perhaps you can do even better. We mustn't spare the expense."

"No," I said, "you've got twenty pounds to spend, haven't you?"

He smiled good-humouredly. "I shall need that on my travels."

"How *is* the ankle?" I said.

"Coming along very nicely. I've been bathing it—in the well! As you see, I'm getting about much better—and when Miss Bourne has fixed the bandage for me it'll no doubt be easier still. Another two days, and you'll be celebrating my departure. . . . And now, Mr. Curtis, I think you'd better be getting back. Miss Bourne and I have had quite a tiring day."

"It looks as though you need a new lamp battery," I said.

"Yes, I was going to mention that. Please don't forget it. And I'd like some cigarettes, I'm running out. *Not* cork-tipped, if you don't mind."

I said, "Is there anything you'd like, Mollie?"

"You might change my library book!" she said.

"I'll bring some papers, anyway." I stood looking at her. I didn't want to leave her. I didn't want to leave either of them. I wanted to have a crack at Smith. But he was at the other side of the roof and I couldn't think of any excuse to get near him.

"Well, good night, Mr. Curtis," he said.

I didn't move.

"I said 'Good night, Mr. Curtis.' "

I still didn't move. I'd suddenly had a very simple idea. I didn't say anything, either. I just stood there.

After a moment he got up and came hobbling over to me. "Are you deaf?" he said, and for the first time that night his voice had a nasty edge. "Get going!" I felt the gun in my ribs.

He looked as though he knew I was up to something, but he didn't know what. His face was about a foot away. The position was perfect. I wondered if he'd have time to press the trigger before the pepper got him. Anyway, I had to take a chance. I said, "I'm sorry, Smith—I've got a frightful pain in my chest." I clapped my hand on my jacket and the pepper shot out.

It missed him completely. The nozzle must have turned, because the spray went sideways instead of upwards. Smith jerked back. The gun was still pointing at me menacingly and his finger was steady on the trigger. He didn't even sneeze. But I did—for a moment or two I was quite helpless. It would have been comic if there hadn't been so much at stake. As it was, it was just a ghastly fiasco.

He waited till I'd stopped sneezing. Then he made me move to a new place, and came up close again and unbuttoned my jacket and took away the insufflator.

"An ingenious idea, Mr. Curtis," he said, "but you really shouldn't have done it, you know. I did warn you. It seems you need another lesson. Stand back!"

He began to hobble towards Mollie. I caught a glimpse of her face in the light as he turned the lamp towards her with his foot. She looked distraught with fear. "Don't!" she breathed. "Oh, please don't!"

I couldn't bear it. Not again. I said, "Smith, if you touch her I swear you'll have to kill me. And that'll be the end of you, too." I took a step towards him, and another. "So help me, I mean it."

He stopped, and gazed at me for a long moment.

"I believe you do," he said. "The breaking point, eh? Well, in that case you'll have to take your own punishment."

He came up to me and stuck the gun hard in my stomach and

gave me a savage punch with his knuckles. He knew just where to hit so that it hurt most—and where he hit was well below the belt. He kept on hitting me, very calmly, very scientifically, and every blow brought its own peculiar agony. I slumped against the wall, as wave after wave of pain passed through me. I knew I couldn't take much more. I was vaguely aware of gasps and cries from Mollie, but they seemed to grow fainter. I *couldn't* take any more. Then the blows suddenly ceased, and I swam slowly back to full consciousness through a haze of pain.

"Well, I think that will do for now," I heard Smith saying. "After all, if I incapacitate you entirely I shan't get those cigarettes. Good night, Mr. Curtis."

I didn't look at Mollie. I couldn't bear to. I knew what she must be feeling, because I'd felt the same the night before. There couldn't be anything much worse than watching someone else being brutally hurt when you couldn't raise a finger to stop it. I said, "Good night, Mollie," and stumbled out through the door.

Chapter Fourteen

The only consolation I took away from the castle that night was that I'd stood up to Smith over Mollie—and won. I knew now that I could prevent him from hurting her. I knew also that, whatever passing torments he might inflict on me, he wouldn't risk doing me any crippling injury. Our relationship, if it could be called that, had reached a point of balance. But I was still no nearer getting that gun away from him—and I was one day nearer the moment of his departure, the final reckoning.

The real problem, of course, was the tower. If Smith had been spending his nights in the courtyard, or even in the first-floor room, there might have been some possibility of creeping in quietly and catching him off guard. But the tower was a safe fortress. It wasn't even as though the door giving access to the roof was a light affair, that I could fling open and rush through. Its heavy oak was inches thick, and he probably kept his foot wedged against it all night. He'd always be ready for me long before I could do anything effective.

In fact, there was really only one way of approaching that roof without announcing my arrival, and that was from the outside of the castle. But how could it be done? Theoretically, I supposed, it might be possible to get hold of a sixty-foot ladder and float it out across the moat and mount it on some improvised raft and climb up—but it would be a difficult operation and certainly not a quiet one. And how could I hope to get a sixty-foot ladder to the castle without attracting dangerous attention in the village? Single-handed, the whole thing was beyond me. The ladder was

out. And the walls were much top smooth to scale without a ladder
. . .

Or were they? I'd rather taken that for granted, but I hadn't
seen them close to—I'd only seen them across the moat. It might
be worth while to examine them more carefully. I had a pair of
binoculars in the car, and I decided to go along to the castle next
day and do a bit of reconnoitring.

Directly after breakfast I collected the glasses from the car boot
and walked up to the kissing-gate. The gate itself was out of sight
of the square tower, but parts of the path were not, and I didn't
want to risk being seen by Smith if I could help it. I debated the
best route to take. Fifty yards to the left, away from the path, there
was a small copse. I could reach that without showing myself.
After that there was a dip in the ground that would give me
adequate cover for most of the way. At the far end I shouldn't be
able to avoid crossing an open space, visible from the tower if
anyone was looking, but the distance was short enough to risk a
quick dash. Beyond the gap, the fringe of hazel bushes beside the
moat would give me cover. Once I'd reached them, I could work
my way round unobserved until I was opposite the tower.

I climbed quickly to the copse and went through it and dropped
down into the dip. I negotiated that, crouching low, and in a few
moments I came to the edge of the gap. I lay down in the grass
and turned my binoculars on the still distant tower. Presumably
Smith had taken Mollie down into the courtyard by now but he
wasn't the sort of chap to count on immunity just because he had
walls around him and I felt sure he would return to the tower
from time to time to have a look round. It was these possible visits
that I was concerned about.

I kept the glasses on the tower for a full ten minutes, but I
couldn't detect any movement at all. I scrutinised all the loopholes,
but there was no sign of anyone there either. It seemed safe to
cross to the hazels. I put my head down, and clutched the binoculars
tight, and made a bolt for it. I was across in seconds. I had another
look at the tower, but there was still no movement.

I began to move slowly round the moat, always keeping the

bushes between me and the tower. It was the first time I'd walked round the edge. I'd gone only a few yards when I came across what looked like an old pontoon in the water. It was a shallow box, about five feet square, moored against the bank among the lilies. It was roughly made and pretty rotten, but it still floated. Probably, I thought, it had been used for fishing. I pulled it in cautiously, until it was concealed by the bushes, and tried my weight on it. There was very little freeboard, and water began to seep in ominously through the bottom, but I thought it would get me over to the wall if I ever wanted to go.

I crept on through the hazel bushes until I was directly opposite the front face of the tower. I sat down on the bank, and through a gap in the leaves I set to work to study the wall in earnest. The glasses were powerful, and I could see every crevice. And there *were* crevices. At close quarters the ancient stone was pocked with irregularities. With a growing sense of excitement I followed them up from the water, noting possible finger holds and toe holds, and they took me right to the top. But there, my imaginary climb struck an insuperable obstacle—the overhang. The five stone corbels which carried the parapet on that side sloped sharply outwards. There were spaces between the corbels, shaped like small arches, into which I might climb. But above them was the protruding parapet itself, and I could see at a glance that those last few feet were beyond the skill of any unaided climber.

However, my hopes had been aroused, and I wasn't in the mood to abandon the project lightly. The tower, jutting out into the moat some fifteen feet from the main wall, had three approachable faces and I worked my way back through the hazels to have a look at one of the sides. I saw at once that the architecture was different. There were only four corbels instead of five. Where the fifth should have been, a section of the tower wall rose straight above the main battlements. If I could climb up near the angle there'd be nothing to prevent me reaching the top.

I turned my glasses on the wall near the angle—and my spirits sank. There were one or two footholds, but nothing like enough to provide a way up. The stonework there seemed less weathered.

I studied the main wall, forty feet high, between the square tower and the round one at the corner of the castle. If I could reach the battlements at any point, I might still make it. But again I failed to find a route. I switched the glasses back to the side of the square tower and inspected the surface near the angle where it joined the front face, and that looked more hopeful. But here, again, I should be stopped by the overhang.

Then I had another idea. The iron slats that had been put in to guard the gap must run along the top of the arches between the corbels. If I could reach them, and get a firm handhold, I could probably swing my way over each corbel in turn until I came to the point where the overhang stopped. In fact, I felt pretty certain that I could. Whether I could do it silently was another matter. But I knew now that I had to make the attempt.

It would have to be done, of course, in daylight. That meant running risks over and above those of the climb itself, for the job might take an hour or more and I'd be pretty conspicuous clinging to the wall—from above, if anyone happened to look down, and from the fields around, if anyone chanced to be passing. But those risks could be reduced by starting early. Crack of dawn was clearly the time, when there'd be no one about and—with luck—Smith would still be dozing.

I gave the surface of the tower wall a final, detailed scrutiny, memorising each of the holds so that the route was fixed in my mind like a photograph. Then I crept back through the bushes, whipped across the gap, and dropped down to the kissing-gate. I had a lot to do.

I collected the Riley from the pub and drove quickly up to London. I had a little flat on a top floor in Chancery Lane and I went straight there. I got out my climbing-boots, and an old windcheater that I always used on climbs because it had a smooth surface and wasn't likely to catch on anything. I also found two flat bits of wood that would do for paddles.

I lunched well away from Fleet Street, and in the afternoon I drove back to the Castle Arms. I asked if there had been any messages for me, but there hadn't. It looked as though my letter to Blair had done the trick as far as the office was concerned.

I decided that I'd have to skip my regular visit to the castle that night. Smith would wonder what had happened to me, but he wasn't likely to do anything drastic just because I'd failed to turn up once. He'd be annoyed not to get his cigarettes and the new battery, but at least there was plenty of food and water at the tower for one more day. And if I was going to be in good condition for that climb, I needed sleep—a long night's sleep.

I turned in soon after dinner and slept soundly until three, the waking hour I'd mentally appointed. I put on my climbing-boots and laced them up tightly, stuck my trouser bottoms into my socks, zipped up the windcheater and crept downstairs. It was still quite dark. I let myself out and walked slowly up the hill to the kissing-gate, with the wooden paddles under my arm. The air was soft, the morning was fine, and there was almost no wind. Climbing conditions should be perfect. I felt exhilarated at the prospect of action, and not unhopeful.

I reached the pontoon, and sat down to wait for daylight. Slowly, the old grey pile emerged from the shadows. It had never seemed more serene and beautiful. A line of someone's verse came into my mind—"Look thy last on all things lovely every hour." For all I knew, I was looking my last on the castle. If I slipped and fell into the moat from sixty feet with these heavy nailed boots on, I didn't give much for my chances. But desperation left no room for fear—and at any moment now I was going to be much too occupied to worry.

I watched the paling sky. The first faint trace of blue was beginning to show. I turned my glasses on the tower roof, but there was nothing visible—and nothing audible. Except for the twittering of birds, the first stirring of the dabchicks at the water's edge, everything was still.

Half past four! This was the moment. I stepped gingerly into the pontoon and untied the painter and pushed off. The water began to seep in at once and I watched it anxiously. It was rising fast but not, I thought, dangerously. It shouldn't take me long to reach the castle. Very quietly, I lowered the paddles into the water. The pontoon proved to be shockingly unmanœuvrable, and I turned two complete circles before I got any sort of control over it. I hadn't reckoned on that. But the knack soon came, and I began to make progress. I didn't dare to hurry—silence was vital. The water lilies were a nuisance, slowing the boat and tangling with the paddles, but I found narrow leads among them and pressed on. In two or three minutes I had reached the wall. There was nothing to tie up to, but on this windless day I thought the pontoon would rest quietly where I left it. Anyway, with a bit of luck I wouldn't need it again. I manœuvred it to the foot of the face that I was going to climb, and looked up. I could see daylight through the slats, sixty feet above me. They looked a hell of a way away! I stood up in the pontoon, steadying myself against the rough wall. I had the feeling that my platform might sink under me at any moment, but I didn't care any more. I found my first fingerhold and my first toehold, and tested them both. Then I pulled myself gently clear of the pontoon. I was off!

Chapter Fifteen

The first few feet were easy. There were two good toeholds in broken stone and a deep crevice to get my fingers into and almost at once I was able to pull myself up to the first loophole. It wasn't the usual slit, it was a small round aperture, just big enough to take my boot. I stood there comfortably and examined the wall above my head. The going looked pretty good as far as the second loophole, which was about halfway up the tower. The holds I had noted through the glasses were even better at close quarters. I continued to climb, slowly and steadily, relying on my feet for upward progress and using the handholds as anchors. There were plenty of handholds, where old mortar had fallen from between the courses of the stones, but good toeholds were rarer. I owed most of them, I imagined, to some ancient bombardment, that had chipped out lumps of solid stone.

I approached the middle loophole with more than a climber's care, for it gave access to the first-floor room of the tower and I couldn't be certain that Smith had made no change in his sleeping-arrangements. I raised myself cautiously till my eyes were level with the bottom of it, and peered in. But it was all right—the room was empty. I drew myself up and got a foot in the loophole and rested again. I had been on the wall for twelve minutes. I glanced around, across the moat to the broad surrounding fields—but only to make sure there was no one about. "Keep your eye on the ball and to hell with the scenery!" is a pretty sound climbing adage—and the only panorama I was interested in at that moment was the view of Smith's face when he didn't have his gun any more.

I inspected the wall again, and there was a pitch ahead that I didn't at all like the look of now that I was near it. One essential toehold was no more than a rough granite edge where a sliver of stone had weathered and sliced off. I'd be all right if it held, but I didn't feel too sure that another bit might not slice off, too, under my weight. Still, it was either that or back to the water. I pressed on, and got a foot firmly in place, and heaved myself up. It seemed all right. I found a deep crack for my right hand, moved my right foot to a new hold and, with relief, took my weight from the dubious one.

Then, suddenly, it happened. The new toehold just disintegrated and in a second I was hanging by my hands alone. I was so close to the wall that I couldn't look down. I could find no place for my toes anywhere. The situation had become a bit desperate. At that moment I'd have given a good deal to know that I had a reliable leader above me, with a nice length of rope and a good anchorage.

I looked along to the right, and there were a couple of fairish toeholds about eight feet away, almost in the middle of the face. From there, upwards, it didn't look too bad. The problem was to reach them. The only way was by a hand-traverse along the crack between the courses, and I started to work my way slowly along it. After a moment I found a hollow as big as an eggcup, that made a very firm hold for fingers, and when I'd passed it and got my left hand there I took my whole weight for a moment on the one hand while I poked out some loose mortar with the fingers of the other. I was nearly there now. I shifted along a bit farther, and found the new toehold, and the second one, and breathed again. I pressed close to the wall, getting the maximum friction hold from my clothes, and relaxed a little. My arms, constantly raised in a way that impeded circulation, were beginning to feel the strain badly.

Still, I hadn't much farther to go, and I felt reasonably confident. As a technical feat, the climb didn't amount to much. Certainly, compared with the four hundred feet of the Eagle's Nest Arête, the almost vertical, well-nigh ledgeless buttress in the Lakes that I'd climbed for fun at Easter, it was child's play. The only thing was, there hadn't been a man with a gun at the top of the Eagle's Nest!

Soon I set off again. Inch by inch and foot by foot I worked my way delicately upwards, moving gradually over to the left until I was almost in a vertical line with my starting point. In a few moments I had reached the third and last of the loophole slits. I was only a foot or two now from the bottom of the parapet.

I listened, but I couldn't hear anything. No limping steps, no sounds of talk. I was too early for them. I climbed a little farther and got a foothold in the loophole and looked up. My fingers were only a few inches from the iron slats. I squeezed myself between two of the corbels and made a final effort and gripped one of the slats. I had a bit of a shock as I put my weight on it, because it was much springier than I'd expected and sagged a bit in the middle. But I was all right—I'd made it!

Now I had to work my way past the jutting corbels to the part of the wall that was clear. The brackets looked bigger and more formidable close to, and I could see they were going to take some negotiating. I squeezed up against the first one, swinging on one hand like a monkey from a branch, and passed my other hand round the protruding stonework, groping for the next bit of slat. I just managed to reach it. I took a firm hold, and drew myself round the face of the stone. Good! If I could pass one, I could pass them all. I looked up again—and suddenly I froze.

Smith was slumped against the parapet, immediately over my head. He was lying at an odd angle, presumably so that he could still reach the door with his foot. From the almost imperceptible movement of his body, I judged him to be asleep or dozing. I could see an area of trouser, and a bit of blanket, and an inch or so of hairy wrist. I pulled myself up as high as I could into the arch between the corbels, and I saw that his right hand was in his trouser pocket. What was more, so was his gun! I could just see the butt.

I felt far more agitated at that moment than at any time on the way up—for I could reach it! This was my opportunity; my first real chance, and probably my last. If I could get it away without disturbing him, and reach the roof before he woke, our worries would be over. But getting it was going to be ticklish. I drew myself up as high as possible with my left hand and cautiously inserted my right hand between the slats. The butt of the gun wasn't clear of the pocket; it would need easing. I felt like a man de-fusing an unexploded mine. One touch on that wrist could set everything off. I got two fingers on the butt and pressed them together in a pinching movement and tried, very gently, to draw out the gun. There was resistance; the corner of the pocket was still holding it. I didn't know whether to go on trying to ease it out, or make one quick grab which would be disastrous if it failed. I tried easing it again, but it wouldn't come. I'd have to grab! If I succeeded, I'd have to disable him with the gun before he had a chance to get at Mollie and start mauling her. I had no choice.

By now the pull on my left arm was almost unendurable. I grasped the slat with my right hand, to ease the pressure for a moment, and let go with my left—and somewhere along the roof there was a sharp, metallic twang. In an instant, Smith was wide awake, with the gun in his hand. He gazed around uncertainly. I heard him go over to Mollie's corner, and come back again. He leaned out over the parapet. Then he glanced down—and saw me. At first he looked quite incredulous. Then an evil grin spread slowly over his face.

"Well!" he said, "if it isn't Mr. Curtis! Another cat burglar, eh?—and a very accomplished one, too. You know, I'm almost inclined to offer you a partnership. This is most amusing."

It didn't amuse me. I felt like hell. I felt worse than I'd ever felt in my life.

I said, "I can't hang on here for ever, Smith. What happens now?"

He swung the gun playfully. "How about a rap or two on the knuckles, Mr. Curtis?" He brought the butt down on the back of my left hand, not hard, but very painfully. I had to loosen my grip.

"If you do that again," I said, "I shall fall."

"So I imagine. Perhaps a swim will cool your ardour for these adventures."

"I'm wearing climbing-boots," I said. "I'm pretty tired. I'll never get ashore if I fall. And if I don't, you won't."

He grinned. "You think of everything." He put the gun back in his pocket.

I said, "Can I come up?"

"How would you get out of the castle door?"

I'd forgotten the door. It was locked, of course, and the key wouldn't unlock it from the inside. "Then I'll have to climb down again," I said.

"I'm afraid so. I'm sorry Miss Bourne can't come and wish you good morning—she's still wired up. But I'll release her in time to see something of your descent. I'm sure she'll be most impressed by your skill."

I began to move back past the corbel on the left.

"Perhaps," he said, following me along, "now that you'll be less busy you'll find time to bring those cigarettes to-night. I get in a very bad temper when I can't smoke. And we're almost out of water."

"I'll be along," I said.

I found the first loophole with my foot, and rested. I wasn't at all looking forward to the climb down. Not that a descent is actually worse than an ascent, but all the hope and excitement had gone out of the day. I was a broken army in retreat. Still, you can't descend a sheer wall with half your mind, and I forced myself to concentrate again on the job. Once, when I looked up, I caught sight of Mollie's face, peering through the slats. It was rigid with horror. I didn't look again.

I had no difficulty in remembering the holds. They were etched in my mind as deeply as in the wall itself. I managed the hand-traverse successfully, negotiated the dangerous bit where the granite had broken away, and reached the middle loophole. The rest was easy. Ten minutes later I was lowering myself into the pontoon. Relieved of my weight, it had made very little more water. I sloshed out a few gallons with my hands, and paddled slowly off through the water lilies. It sank under me as I touched the bank.

Chapter Sixteen

I spent most of that day frantically trying to devise some new plan. Judging by the way Smith had moved about the roof on waking, it couldn't be long now before he was ready to leave. Not to-night, I thought, but almost certainly the next night. That gave us only thirty-six hours before the final crisis. The feeling of desperate urgency didn't help constructive thinking, and I made little progress. Smith would obviously be keeping the closest watch on the walls from now on, so there wasn't a hope that I could get away with a second attempt at scaling them. Surprise up the spiral staircase remained impossible. That seemed to rule out any chance of successful night activity.

I wondered if the courtyard in daylight might offer any prospects. There was quite a lot of cover there, and nothing to prevent me staying on there, instead of leaving, after I'd delivered the next lot of supplies. Then, when Smith and Mollie came down at daybreak, I might be able to catch Smith unawares. But when I thought about it in detail, I realised how little likelihood there was of that. He would certainly have the possibility well in mind. Unless I was very much mistaken he would come out of the bottom door of the tower using Mollie as a shield. And once out, he would do what anyone in his position would do—he would go straight over to the main gate and make sure it was locked. If it was, he would know I had left. If it wasn't, he would know I hadn't, and he'd stalk me with his gun. In daylight I wouldn't have a chance.

I tried to think of some way of getting him down into the courtyard at night, some trick that wouldn't look like a trick, but I couldn't. I could scarcely think at all any more. I found myself going over and over the same ground, in a state of mind that at times wasn't far short of panic. I reached only one decision. If, by the next day, the situation still looked quite hopeless, I would go to the police and tell them everything. There was just an outside chance that they might be able to suggest something—and by then, we'd have nothing more to lose. If we were going to be killed in any case, at least I might as well make sure that Smith didn't get away with it. It wouldn't be much consolation, but it would be something.

I went into Brighton again before lunch and did some more shopping. I got the battery, and a batch of newspapers and magazines for Mollie, and the cigarettes and a bottle of wine to sweeten Smith, and another water can and a little food. After that I returned to Lodden and parked the Riley behind the tea-house and settled down at the pub for another ghastly wait.

When I finally reached the castle just after midnight, the routine was exactly the same as on the first occasion. I knocked at the top door and was cautiously admitted with my hands up, and very efficiently searched. Smith asked me if I'd brought the battery and I said I had and he told me to put it in the lamp, which by now was giving out such a feeble glow that I could scarcely see Mollie at all. He stood over me while I made the transfer, digging the gun into me. He was putting much more pressure on his ankle to-night, no doubt because it was firmly bandaged. I knew I'd been right—the final show-down couldn't be far away.

Directly I'd got the lamp fixed I went over to Mollie. She was sitting on one of the blankets with her back to the parapet. She was still wired to the slats.

I said to Smith, "Do you have to keep her fastened up like this even when you're not asleep?"

"Only when you're here," Smith said. "She's been free since dusk. ... As a matter of fact, Miss Bourne and I are getting along very well. I think we understand each other. If I may say so, she has a much more realistic approach to the situation than you have."

I bent over her. "How do you feel, Mollie?"

"All right," she said. Her voice was very subdued; she sounded pretty beaten. I scarcely recognised in her the spirited girl I'd known before Smith had come on the scene.

I said, "I'm sorry I didn't manage to pull off that climb this morning."

She raised her head, and for the first time that night I saw her face clearly. Astoundingly, it wore an expression of furious anger. "It was idiotic to try," she burst out. "You must be crazy."

I was completely taken aback. I said, "Well, I had to do something."

"Why? If you're trying to impress me with your bravery, I can tell you you're not succeeding. Don't you realise how dangerous it was?"

I shrugged. "I got down all right, so why worry?"

"As it happens, I wasn't thinking of you—if you want to break your neck that's your affair. But you might have got us both killed. Why don't you stop fooling about and just wait?"

"You see what I mean?" Smith said. "Miss Bourne has sense."

I ignored him. "Wait for what?" I said grimly.

"Mr. Smith says he's almost ready to leave, and as far as I'm concerned, he can. I know what he's done, and I know it means he's going to get away with murder, but it's not our job to stop him—we're not the police. I'm certainly not prepared to sacrifice myself to do it. I want to live, do you understand? *Live!*" Her face shone white and scared in the lamplight, her voice was touched with hysteria. "So for God's sake stop behaving like an overgrown boy scout."

I could scarcely believe my ears. It seemed incredible that Mollie could be so naïve as to think Smith would leave us behind alive. It was on the tip of my tongue to tell her he'd be bound to kill us before he went, but I didn't want to put my certainty into words for him to hear. And anyway, I'd scarcely the heart. She must have had a fearful time, shut up here alone with a sadist and a murderer for days and nights on end, never quite knowing what he might do next. Her ordeal had been immeasurably worse than mine, and if the strain had got her down I couldn't justly blame her. I certainly didn't want to say anything to make things worse for her—she'd learn the brutal truth soon enough.

All the same, I couldn't help feeling let down. Her boasted toughness hadn't even been skin-deep. As a hard-boiled reporter she was a fake. She was just a fair-weather girl. I remembered again how she'd folded up at the sight of Hoad's body; how she'd cringed in terror when Smith had approached her corner to strike her; and now this! She'd been ready enough to get into this scrape—to get me into it, too, for that matter!—but now that things had gone wrong she couldn't take it. Still, there it was. I'd have to count her out in anything else I attempted—and in the long run it probably wouldn't make any difference. The long run? Twenty-four hours!

I said, in a bitter tone, "Well, you needn't worry—I'm hardly in a position to try anything else." I turned to Smith. "Just give me your instructions. What do you want me to do?"

He gave a sardonic grin. "Nothing that will tax you at all, Mr. Curtis. Your work's nearly over. . . . Tell me, where's your car?"

"Down by the gate."

"Does it run well?"

"Very well."

"How much petrol is there in the tank?"

I remembered that I'd meant to fill up that afternoon, and hadn't. "About a gallon, I should think."

"How many miles is that good for?"

"Something between twenty and twenty-five."

"H'm!—that's not going to be much help. All right—now here's what you must do. Some time during the day, get the tank filled right up. Check the oil and water at the same time. As soon as darkness falls, bring the car back and park it where it is now. See that the ignition key is left in, and that the doors are unlocked. Then come up here. That's all."

"I gather you're going to take my car," I said.

"I'm going to borrow it—just for a few hours. I shall leave it quite intact—and no doubt the police will return it to you eventually."

"I see. . . . And what are your plans for us?"

"Well, now, as far as you're concerned, Mr. Curtis, I shall leave you locked up here in the castle. You'll have a little food and water, so you'll be quite all right. As for Miss Bourne, I'm afraid I shall have to ask her to go along with me as a hostage for a little while longer. She will be my guarantee against any monkey business at the car. It would be so easy, otherwise, for you to organise a police ambush down there by the gate, wouldn't it? I'm sure you'd already thought of it! This way, you won't dare to organise anything—because, in the last resort, you will know that I should kill her. I still have nothing to lose."

I said, "When will you let her go?"

"As soon as I'm safely away from here. I may have to leave her tied up somewhere for an hour or two, to make sure I have plenty of time to get out of the country before the police pick up my trail—but then she's used to that, by now! You needn't worry, I shall treat her well. In the end, of course, she'll be found, and she'll raise the alarm, and then you'll be liberated, too. I think you'll agree that all my arrangements are extremely considerate."

"Is that all?" I said.

"That's all. You can go, now."

I glanced at Mollie. She didn't look angry any more. She just looked very troubled. She said, "Hugh, I'm sorry if I seemed ungrateful just now. I'm afraid I must have done, horribly. I don't know what you must be thinking of me . . ." Her voice broke. "I couldn't help it, I just couldn't bear the thought of any more violence. It's been such a ghastly nightmare, you can't imagine . . ." Suddenly, she began to cry.

"Easy, there!" Smith called out sharply. "We don't want the neighbourhood roused."

She tried to check her weeping, but now that she'd begun she couldn't stop. "I'm so—*tired*," she sobbed. "I'm so uncomfortable. This beastly wire's cutting my foot."

Smith grunted, and got up. "I can soon fix that for you. . . . Just stand back a minute, Mr. Curtis. Right back!"

I stood back. There was still no chance of getting the gun. I felt very low, and terribly inadequate. I gazed out over the faintly starlit countryside, thinking how peaceful it all looked, thinking again how utterly incredible this whole thing was . . .

Then, suddenly, all hell broke out. Mollie yelled, "Hugh!" at the top of her voice. I swung round in astonishment. She'd got Smith by the hair with both hands. I dived across the roof. As I reached them they rolled over together. For a moment I couldn't distinguish anything. There was a whirl of flailing arms and legs. The lamp was turned away—I couldn't see where to hit, what to hold. Then there was a blow, and a cry, and Smith suddenly tore himself away and I felt the hard barrel of the gun against me. "Breathe and you're dead!" he said.

It was all over. The whole incident hadn't taken more than ten seconds. Mollie was lying back against the parapet, holding her face. Smith was sucking his left hand, which was covered with blood.

"You little hellcat!" he said.

I kept very still. "Careful, Smith!" I said. "No reprisals!—not if you want me to live, that is. Not if you need my car."

He stepped back, still sucking his hand. "You'd better go, Mr. Curtis."

"Go on, Hugh," Mollie said. She had got over the blow—she didn't appear to be seriously damaged. "He won't hurt me now."

I said, "Sorry, Mollie!"

"You needn't be. It was a long shot—like climbing the wall. It might have worked."

She smiled, and gave me a gallant little wave, and I walked slowly to the steps.

Chapter Seventeen

As I crossed the courtyard, I called myself every name under the sun. I'd been unforgivably dim not to see through that act that Mollie had been putting on. I ought to have known that she couldn't be that naïve. I ought to have had more faith in her as an ally. If I'd been prepared for some sudden move, if I'd been on my toes, we might just have got away with it. It was *I* who had let *her* down.

Now there was nothing to prevent Smith going right ahead with his escape plans—his real plans. He'd wait for me to bring the car that evening, he'd shoot us both, and he'd disappear. Probably he wouldn't even trouble to dispose of our bodies. All that stuff about locking me up in the castle and taking Mollie with him was merely intended to keep hope alive in us and scare me off a last-minute appeal to the police. I could just imagine him leaving Mollie tied up behind some haystack while he went off to Dover to get the next boat! Suppose she got free before he was ready?—suppose someone found her? It was derisory. If I'd had any doubts before about his murderous intentions, they certainly wouldn't have survived that childish apology for a plan.

I closed the castle door behind me and thrust the key savagely into the lock. When I tried to turn it, it wouldn't turn. I wriggled it about, but it still wouldn't budge. I couldn't understand it, because I'd never had any difficulty with the lock before, not from the outside. The obstruction that had prevented me locking it from the inside must have moved. I strained on the key, hoping to force it past whatever was there, but all I succeeded in doing was jamming it tight. I couldn't move the key now in any direction. The door was still unlocked, and I couldn't lock it.

I stood back and considered the situation, and the more I thought about it the less I liked it. If I left the door as it was, the final crisis might come long before the evening. The day that would soon be dawning was a Saturday—the first Saturday since the news of the murder had got out. It was quite possible that sightseers would come to the castle. Someone might try the door. Someone might go in. And then everything would blow up. I didn't want that to happen. I didn't want to do anything to hasten the end. I was still clinging desperately to shreds of hope—hope of a last-minute miracle.

I had another go at the lock, but I still couldn't move it. In the darkness, I couldn't see what I was doing. A light on the inside would have helped—a light, and something to probe with. A piece of wire might shift the obstruction. Smith had some wire. I'd better go back and tell Smith. He wouldn't want the castle left open, either!

I set off back through the entrance passage. I wondered what he'd say. He'd be bound to suspect some trick—and yet it wasn't a trick. I could probably convince him of that. Truth was very persuasive. And with so much at stake, I didn't see how he could fail to come.

Then a new thought struck me. It wasn't a trick—but maybe I could turn it into one? I tried to visualise what would happen when I told him. He'd make me come down with him, of course. He'd stick close by me on the way down. He'd keep the gun against me all the time. He'd be more careful than ever while we worked on the lock. I doubted if he'd give me any opportunity . . .

If only, I thought, I could let him know what had happened without going back to the tower—if only I could make him come down and join me in the passage . . .

I stopped abruptly. I'd suddenly had an idea. The germ of an idea, anyway. Perhaps I *could* get him to come and join me. If I could, the passage offered wonderful opportunities. Unique opportunities! I stood there in the darkness, trying to work it out.

It was a fantastic plan—but a tremendously exciting one. A long shot, like all the others—but it might come off. And what had I to lose? Smith wasn't the only desperate man now.

First, though, I had to find out if it was practicable. I made my way quickly to the inner end of the passage. Where it entered the courtyard it was flanked, I remembered, by slopes of broken masonry. Those slopes must lead, presumably, to a flat surface above the passage. I felt around and found the bottom of one of the slopes and clambered up. There was no difficulty. In a few seconds I was at the top. It was just as I'd expected—a flattish, rather uneven roof. I daren't strike a match, because I was in full view of the tower, but I groped around with my hands and almost at once I found one of the round holes I was looking for—the murder holes! I continued to feel around. Altogether there were nine of them, and between them they commanded most of the passage. The middle one was larger than the others, but even the smaller ones had a diameter of seven or eight inches. I scraped up a handful of stone fragments and dropped one down each hole in turn, and they all fell clear to the passage below.

I began to search for a heavy piece of stone, something I could use as a weapon, but there didn't seem to be anything loose at all. It was going to be difficult to find a suitable missile in the darkness. I tried to remember where I'd seen bits of stone of a suitable size—and after a moment I did remember. I climbed down over the masonry and left the castle. I crossed the causeway and knelt down on the grass at the side of the moat and felt along the edge. The bank just there had been strengthened with lumps of stone, and some of them were loose. The first bit I dislodged was too big, but the second felt just right. It was a rectangular lump about six inches across at the widest place, and almost a foot long. It must have weighed twenty pounds. I lugged it from its bed and carried it back through the passage and set to work to get it up the slope. It was a slow job, for the tower was well within earshot and I didn't want Smith to hear anything that I couldn't explain afterwards. Any vague noises could be attributed to work on the lock. I made my way up mostly on my hands and knees, keeping the stone in front of me and lifting it upwards and forwards as I advanced. In three or four minutes I had reached the top again. I tried the stone in one of the holes, and it fitted nicely.

I left it there beside the hole and climbed down again and went out through the door. I walked round the moat till I was opposite the square tower. For a second or two I stood listening. Caution had become a habit. But it was two o'clock in the morning and the place couldn't have been more deserted. I didn't think there was a chance that anyone but Smith would hear me. I cupped my hands towards the tower and gave a loud hail.

For a second or two, nothing happened. I was just beginning to think I'd have to shout again when I saw some movement up on the parapet against the background of the stars. Then Smith's voice came clearly over the water. "Yes?—what is it?"

"The lock's jammed," I called. "I've locked the door, but I can't get the key out."

He reacted to that, all right. He had to. If the door had really been locked, and the door jammed, he'd have been a prisoner. He said anxiously, "Any idea what the trouble is?"

"I don't know—there's some obstruction. Maybe you could poke it out from the inside. What about bringing some wire and a light?"

There was a short silence. I didn't even have to guess what he was thinking. Then he called, "All right—I'll come down. But watch your step, Mr. Curtis!"

The stars that had been obscured became visible again. I turned and raced back round the moat. I slipped in quietly through the door and closed it behind me and climbed up again on to the passage roof. I'd scarcely got into position when I saw a glimmer of light at the bottom of the tower steps, and Smith emerged. He came out with infinite caution, pushing the door open an inch at a time. He had the hand lamp in his left hand, the gun in his right. He closed the door behind him and stood for a moment with his back to it, flashing the light around. When he'd made sure I wasn't concealed near by, he began to advance slowly into the courtyard.

I pressed myself down flat against the roof and watched him. He was suspicious, all right—I'd never seen a man behave more circumspectly. He examined every foot of that courtyard. He looked behind every bit of masonry, he flashed his light down the steps to the well, he went into each of the hollow towers in turn. He was obviously worried about his rear. But at last he satisfied himself that I wasn't hiding anywhere, and he moved towards the entrance passage at a slow, stealthy pace. It was the first time I'd seen him walk any distance. He still had a limp, but even with the limp he gave an impression of great agility in reserve.

He was coming straight on, now; straight for the middle of the passage. It looked as though he was going to pass right under the biggest of the murder holes. I raised the stone and lowered it into the hole and concentrated on gauging his speed as he moved under the arch. My heart was pounding so fiercely I could scarcely breathe. I'd lost sight of him now. He was in the passage. Through the hole, I could see the advancing light getting brighter. Another second or two, and he'd be under me. I eased the stone away from the edge of the hole, so that it would fall freely . . .

Then he stopped. He seemed to be shining the light around again. For an awful moment I thought he'd noticed the stone fragments I'd dropped—but the beam had come to rest on one of the side walls. Then I remembered the shallow dungeon that lay on one side of the passage. That was it—he was making sure of his flank. He moved towards the dungeon, away from my line of fire. I drew the stone up and changed my position slightly, so that I had the choice of two holes. But I couldn't see him anymore.

I heard him go into the dungeon and come quickly out again. He seemed to be much jumpier than usual. The light flashed back towards the courtyard. Then, at last, he reached the door. I heard him call out, "Are you there, Mr. Curtis?" For a few seconds there was silence. Then I heard him trying the door handle. One of the doors creaked on its hinges as he slowly opened it. Now he'd *know* that I was up to something, because the door wasn't locked as I'd said it was. But he'd found the jammed key, and he still had his problem. I heard him fiddling with it—I heard the scrape of wire in the lock. Every now and again he stopped and flashed the light around. He must have pretty well closed the door again, I decided, or he wouldn't have dared to show so much light.

The fiddling went on for at least five minutes. He was obviously reluctant to leave the lock jammed, but he didn't seem to be having any success with it. Presently I heard the squeak of the door handle again—he was shutting the door. He must have given up. Once more the beam of light turned inwards. He was coming back through the passage. It was harder to judge his whereabouts, now, but the light gave some indication. He'd still have the gun in his right hand, the lamp in his left. The centre of the beam, therefore, would be about eighteen inches to the left of him. I changed my position again, and chose a third hole. The beam grew stronger. I lowered the stone into the hole. There was a gap between the edge of the stone and the side of the hole, but I couldn't see much through it. I'd have to gamble everything on a guess. He must be almost under me now. . . . I caught a glimpse of the swinging lamp, and a shadow passed beneath me, and I let the stone go.

There was a cry, a crash—and the light went out.

I listened. I couldn't hear a thing. He might be dead. He might be unconscious. Or he might be just shamming, waiting for me to show myself. He was quite capable of it. If I rushed down into the passage and he was shamming I'd have the gun in my ribs in no time. I listened again. I thought I caught a faint sound, but I couldn't identify it. I wasn't even sure where it came from. . . . Suddenly I realised that by far the best course was to make for the tower. Once I was up there with Mollie, and we had that thick top door between us and the gun, Smith would be helpless. I slipped off my shoes and lowered myself, inch by cautious inch, back into the courtyard. Dawn was near, but for the moment the night seemed darker than ever and I couldn't see anything at all. I tried to remember where the various obstructions were that I'd passed so often. I groped my way forward with outstretched hands. Presently I felt grass under my feet and knew I was all right. I quickened my steps, closing in on the tower. My pulse was racing. Even if Smith came rushing up behind me with the gun, I could make a dash for it now—I was near enough. But there was no pursuit. I reached the door and dragged it open and slipped inside. *I'd made it!*

Overwhelming relief surged through me. The miracle had happened. We were going to live after all! I didn't care now whether Smith was lying senseless in the passage or stalking me out there in the courtyard. It made no difference. He'd lost his base, his fortress. There was nothing more he could do.

I raced up the stone spiral. The top door was open. I rushed out on to the roof and heaved the door shut behind me. "Mollie . . .!" I cried exultantly.

A voice from the parapet said, "Stay right where you are, Mr. Curtis! I can see you against the sky."

Chapter Eighteen

The utter unexpectedness of it made it the worst blow yet. I leaned back against the parapet, very near to despair. I could do nothing right, it seemed; Smith could do nothing wrong. He was always one move ahead of me. He obviously thought much faster than I did. He must have recovered himself the instant the stone had fallen, and sized the situation up and nipped back to the tower noiselessly while I was still wondering if he was dead. It had been quite a feat for a limping man, especially in the dark. But then, of course, he was a cat burglar. I'd forgotten that. Perhaps he had cat's eyes, too.

If he had, he wasn't relying on them now. He said, "Keep quite still, Mr. Curtis. I don't want any movement until daylight."

I didn't want any movement, either. I'd half expected him to come over and beat me up again, and it was a relief that he wasn't going to. I relaxed a little, and looked across at Mollie's corner. Now that there was no lamp, I couldn't see her at all. I said, "Are you wired up, Mollie?"

"Yes. He did it before he went down. . . . What happened?"

I told her.

Smith said, with mock indignation, "He might have killed me!" He sounded very pleased with himself. No one would have thought that twenty pounds of granite had just missed his head by centimetres. He was a diabolical villain, and I hated his guts, but he wasn't entirely contemptible.

Mollie said, "Better luck next time!"

After that we were quiet for a bit. The sky in the east grew lighter. The blackness above slowly paled to grey. I could just see

Smith, now, lying back against the parapet with his gun at the ready. And Mollie, too, blanketed like a squaw, very still, very watchful. She hadn't given up, I felt sure—not by a long chalk.

When it was light enough to see clearly, Smith got up and motioned me to the door with his gun. "I'll come and collect my footwear, too," he said. I hadn't noticed before that he was shoeless.

I said "Good-bye" to Mollie once more. I seemed always to be saying "Hallo" or "Good-bye." I had a feeling that this time it might be a long farewell, that when I returned to the castle with the car, Smith would kill me before I saw her—but I mentally shrugged off the thought.

I went down the stairs a step ahead of Smith, with the gun in my back. I crossed the courtyard, still in front of him. When we reached the entrance passage he climbed part of the way up the broken masonry with me so that he could keep me covered while I put my shoes on. In the passage, he made me stand facing the door while he put his own shoes on. He picked up the battered, useless lamp and tossed it into the dungeon. He didn't seem to mind not having it any more. No doubt he thought he could kill us in the dark just as easily as in the light.

I said, "What about the door? Anyone could come in, now."

He fingered the gun, almost lovingly. "It'll be too bad if anyone does. Still, we don't want unnecessary trouble, do we? Perhaps you'd better get the stone shot, Mr. Curtis."

I walked over to the bombard. Smith came with me. He was taking no chances of a breakaway to the tower. He didn't lower his gun even after I'd lifted the shot, though he could safely have done so. It was a hell of a weight. I staggered to the passage with it and dropped it a foot or two from the door with a sigh of relief.

Smith grinned. "I carried it farther than that!" he said, and waited. "Well, push it against the door."

I looked at him in surprise. "Aren't I going to leave?" I said.

He shook his head. "I've changed my plans. You can leave this afternoon."

"What's the idea?"

"I'm getting a little tired of your tricks, Mr. Curtis. You're altogether too inventive. I prefer to keep you under my eye as long as possible."

"Just as you like," I said. I rolled the shot against the door.

"Right," he said. "Now we'll get back to the tower."

We crossed the courtyard again in single file—myself, the gun, and Smith. On the spiral staircase he was still only one step behind me. Mollie looked surprised to see me back. She asked what the change of plan was for, and Smith told her. He threw me a blanket and told me to sit down with my back to the parapet. There was a draught coming up through the slats, he said, and he wouldn't like me to catch a chill! I sat down. Presently Mollie asked if she could go and stretch her legs and he said she could but she wasn't to go outside the castle in case some villager happened to be around early and recognised her. He limped across and released her from the wire. He seemed to be quite confident he could trust her, as long as he held me as a hostage.

The sun was up, now, and the warmth was comforting. I sat and watched Smith gently massaging his ankle. It still seemed to be giving him a bit of trouble. I asked him if we should all be going down into the courtyard later, and he grinned and said he didn't think so, not now the castle doors were unlocked. We'd just have to be very careful not to show our heads, he said—for all our sakes! It was depressing news, because there might have been some opportunity for manœuvre in the courtyard, some chance of a diversion. Up here, there was none.

It felt strange being a prisoner on the roof, with Mollie free down below. This must be about the first time, I thought, that she'd really been off the leash. I wondered what she was thinking, what sort of ideas she was turning over in her mind. I wondered how long she'd be. . . . Then I suddenly had a new idea of my own. Perhaps I could shake Smith's faith in Mollie! If I could rattle him enough, he might do something stupid. I picked up one of the papers I'd brought the night before and pretended to glance through it, because I didn't want him to think I was planning anything. I let a full minute pass. Then I looked down through the slats—and gave a startled exclamation.

I said, "Miss Bourne doesn't seem to be as obedient as I am."

"What do you mean?"

"I thought you told her not to leave the castle. She's just gone down to the river."

Smith looked pretty startled, too. He came over and peered through the slats himself. He said, "I don't see her."

"She's down the slope. It was her, all right."

He gazed at me suspiciously. "Now what are you up to?"

"I'm not up to anything," I said, "but I'm just wondering if she is. I'm not sure you haven't been a bit too trusting, Smith."

"Nonsense! She knows very well what'll happen to you if she tries anything. She wouldn't want her boy friend shot."

"I'm not her boy friend, unfortunately. I only met her three days ago. She doesn't give a damn about me."

"I didn't get that impression."

I gave a derisive laugh. "I wouldn't have thought you'd have trusted your impressions, after what happened the other night. She's a tough baby, that girl. She'd sell her own flesh and blood for a story. Anyway, she probably doesn't believe you'd shoot me when it came to it. I'd say you've had it, Smith. I think she's gone for the police."

"Well, I don't," he said—but he was looking a bit worried, all the same. "I don't believe she's left the castle. What about the stone shot?"

"Anyone could roll that away, from the inside. I tell you I saw her."

"I don't think you did."

I shrugged. "You'll see. I'll take an even bet the police will be here inside half an hour."

"Then that's just how long you've got to live, Mr. Curtis!"

"I don't see why you should take it out of me," I said. "I've been let down more than you have. You deserve it, I don't. Besides, I thought you were interested in escape, not revenge. You could be out of here in a jiffy. My car's at the gate—there's enough petrol to take you out of the neighbourhood. I know it's not what you planned, but it's something."

"Very thoughtful of you," he said. "But I should still kill you before I went. I'm a man of my word!"

"It's up to you," I said. "Personally, I'd have thought it was stupid. You'd feel fine, wouldn't you, if you met Miss Bourne coming up the path and discovered that she hadn't been to the police after all—and you'd bumped me off for nothing."

He was beginning to look a bit confused. I knew he didn't believe anything I said, but I thought he didn't quite disbelieve it, either. I picked up the paper again and continued to read. He walked to the other side of the roof and looked over, cautiously. After a moment he walked back again. If I'd achieved nothing else, I'd got him really worried at last. Very soon, I thought, he'd take me down into the courtyard with him to make sure. That was the most I'd hoped for. If he had two of us on his mind, in the open, I might still have a chance to get the gun . . .

Then the whole thing fizzled out. There was a step on the spiral staircase. Smith called out sharply, "Who's that?" and Mollie said, "It's me—who do you think?" and came out on to the roof.

Smith gave me a wide grin. "I *thought* I was a better judge of character than that, Mr. Curtis . . ." He didn't bother to tell her what had happened. "Well, now, perhaps Miss Bourne would get us something to eat."

He told her what to get, and where to put it down. Once he reminded her to keep her head away from the parapet. He was very much in control of the situation again, moving us around like pawns. When the food was ready, he ate hungrily. Mollie said she only wanted a drink of water. I thought I'd better make a show of eating, but the food almost choked me. I reckoned we had about twelve hours to live, and it wasn't a thought to give one an appetite. I never had believed that hearty-meal-before-execution stuff, and now I knew it wasn't true.

After breakfast, Smith smoked a cigarette. I asked him if I could smoke, too, but he said No, he didn't want any hot ash flying around. He was getting more and more cautious about not giving me any chances. He even went through the bag of supplies and flung everything over into the moat that I could conceivably use as a weapon. His own hammer and chisel followed the knives and forks and tin opener. By the time he'd finished there was nothing on the roof but two soft bags and a little food, the water can, and a couple of plastic tumblers.

Then he wired Mollie up again. As he refixed the wires to the slats, I heard the twang that had given me away when I'd scaled the wall. I realised now what had made the noise. Each set of slats was bolted down to two of the stone corbels but the ends were free, so that the last four or five feet were merely *supported* by the next corbel. As I'd noticed when I'd put my weight on them from underneath, they were very springy, and when they were released after pressure at any point, they twanged. But for that, I thought ruefully, we probably wouldn't be there now.

As soon as Mollie was well secured, Smith came and sat down beside me—but at a safe distance. It was the spot he always occupied at night, to keep his foot against the door, but I could see that it had other advantages as well. From where he was, he had a clear view through the slats right across to the path that led up from the gate. It was a highly strategic spot in daylight too. By leaning over, I could just share the view. But I still couldn't reach Smith. His hand, with the gun, was outstretched along the slats almost carelessly, or so it seemed, but it was too far away to be any good to me.

We were obviously in for a long wait, now—and an unproductive one. Until Smith made some fresh move, there was nothing I could do. Mollie tried a new tactic—needling him. She called him a lot of names, in a quiet, contemptuous way, and told him he hadn't the slightest chance of escaping the police in the long run—but if her idea was to provoke him into starting something, it didn't work. He just looked at her appreciatively and grinned. Presently she changed her approach and began to ask him about himself, but he didn't respond to that, either. She asked him what his little bag of jewels was worth and he said, "Enough to keep me in luxury for the rest of my life," but that was all. She gave up, then, and switched to me, and we discussed what sort of space the story was likely to get in our papers when we were in the clear again, and she said being with Smith for three days had been the worst experience of her life but that in the end it would probably turn out to have been almost worth it. I don't know whether her chatter deceived Smith or not. He just sat there inscrutably, fingering his gun. We talked about ourselves a bit, rather half-heartedly, because the past isn't very interesting unless there's a future too. We made a few cracks, a sort of proud defiance, boosting each other's morale. Then the talk faded out.

It was just before eleven when Smith, suddenly very alert, announced that two people were walking up the path towards the castle door. I leaned over and caught sight of them just before they went out of view—a man and a girl, with their arms round each other. Smith got up and crossed to the other side of the roof, crouching down, so that he could see over the courtyard to the entrance passage without any risk of being seen himself. I made a tentative move, just to see how great his preoccupation was, but he whipped round in a second and I didn't try it again. His air of amused unconcern had quite gone—his face was as hard as the stone he was leaning against. I hadn't a doubt that if those two forced their way in and came up to the tower, he would kill them without a qualm. And us, too, if he had any trouble. There was no help for us that way—it would merely precipitate the end. For a moment or two we waited in a state of almost unbearable suspense. Then the pair came sauntering round the end of the castle, circled the moat, and walked slowly away.

Another hour passed. Several more people approached the castle, but no one tried to get in. I'd been right about the Saturday sightseers, but I'd under-rated the effect of the "Closed" notice at the gate, which would make most people assume that the castle door was locked. In any case, the stone shot would frustrate any but a most determined effort to get in. Smith hadn't really much to worry about.

As the time dragged slowly by, my spirits ebbed to a new low. Things were no worse than I'd expected them to be, but forced inactivity made them seem worse. We were obviously going to be kept sitting here all day. I could see no prospect of any useful diversion. I could think of nothing to bring about any hopeful change in the situation. There seemed to be two courses open to me, both pretty grim. I could get in touch with the police when I went to fill up the car tank, and that would take care of Smith—but it would mean certain death for Mollie. Or I could try a last reckless dive for the gun. If we were going to be shot anyway, I might as well make a fight of it. Even Smith might not find a fatal spot with the first bullet . . .

I was still reflecting on the desperate alternatives when I heard voices. Several voices. Distant, at first, but getting louder and closer every second. Smith jerked the gun threateningly, and peered through the slats. I leaned over and looked, too. A couple of youths appeared on the path, riding bicycles. Behind them were two girls, also riding. And then, up the slope, so many cyclists came surging that I lost count. There were thirty of them, at least—a whole club. And they were all making for the castle door.

Chapter Nineteen

Smith scrambled to his feet and went over to the ramparts again so that he could watch the entrance passage. I couldn't see the cyclists any more, but I didn't feel this was the moment to change my position. Smith's finger was tight on the trigger of his gun; he was beginning to look like a man with an itch to shoot. Anyway, I didn't need to see, because his expression told me what was happening. These young people didn't give a fig for notice boards—or stone shots behind locked doors that moved at a push. They were coming in! Their cockney voices were suddenly much louder. They were in high, larking spirits. They were flowing over the courtyard in a tidal wave of shouts and laughter.

Smith's face had turned a dirty, mottled colour. An incursion on this scale was something that even he hadn't allowed for.

I said, "This is it, Smith. You've lost, I'm afraid."

"Don't move!" he said. "Don't move an inch!" His expression was vicious. "If I lose, you lose. But don't worry—I'm not finished yet." He tapped his gun meaningly.

"You can't shoot all of them," Mollie exclaimed in a tone of horror. "Why start something you can't finish? You haven't a chance."

"We shall see."

I sat still, listening. I could hear individual voices quite plainly now—even what they were saying. Someone shouted across the courtyard, "These castles look like they just been put 'ere, don't they?" A girl said shrilly, "Get on, you soppy date, I want to see, too." There was more laughter. The tidal wave was sweeping on. They seemed to be down by the well now. One of them called out,

"Prob'ly the bride's barf or somefin'." Another said, "Coo, look what's up 'ere!"

They'd reached the tower. They were certain to come up. I could see no end to it now but a massacre. First us, and then as many of them as there were bullets for.

Suddenly Smith stepped across to Mollie and released her from the wire and jerked her to her feet. "Down the steps!" he said. He turned on me. "You stay here. You know what happens to the girl if you try anything."

He stuck the gun in his pocket, but he was still holding it. The barrel was pointing at Mollie as they went down the steps.

I wasn't at all sure now what he was up to. If he was going to shoot his way out, why hadn't he started with us? Why had he taken Mollie? He must have some other plan. I crossed to the door and stood there listening. He seemed to have stopped half-way down at the first-floor room. I heard him say, "Get in there and keep quiet." That must be to Mollie. I heard the youths and girls come piling up the stairs. Someone was whistling the theme tune from *La Ronde*. A voice said, "Ever see *The Thirty-Nine Steps*, Alf?"

Then I heard Smith again. "What do you people think you're doing?" he demanded in a tone of authority. "Get out, all of you. The castle doesn't open till next month. Can't you read?"

So that was it!

There was a moment's silence—then an outbreak of indignant "Coo's" and a few catcalls. Some bold youth said, "'Oo are you, mister, anyway?"

"I'm the caretaker. Now push off, all of you, or I'll call the police."

There was murmuring at that, and more derisive jeers.

"Go on," Smith said, "before I collect a bob off each of you."

That worked better than the threat. There was a bit of grumbling, a bit of argument. Then, slowly, the tide began to recede. In a moment or two they were all back in the courtyard. There were a few more insults, hurled from safety. There was more laughter. There was a cheeky cacophony of bicycle bells as they collected their machines. Then the noise gradually subsided. They were going. Smith had pulled it off.

I moved to the ramparts and watched them leave the courtyard. They weren't in any hurry. Some of them had begun fooling about on the edge of the moat outside. Smith didn't wait for their final departure. As the last one went out through the door he emerged from the tower with Mollie in front of him and the gun still in his pocket and crossed the courtyard to the entrance passage. He was obviously going to replace the stone shot against the door. In a few moments he'd be back on the roof—and we'd all be as we were again.

I couldn't let that happen. I knew I'd got to do something now. Even though he'd be sure to come back with Mollie ahead of him and the gun in her back, I'd never have a better chance to surprise him. I'd never have the freedom of the roof again. I gazed anxiously round. Suppose I crouched behind the door? No, he'd expect that. *Above* the door, perhaps? There was a little turret over the top of the spiral staircase, and the door opened out of the turret. I could climb up on to it—and try dropping down on him as he came in. But it wasn't much of a place to drop from—there was a lot of fancy stonework, but no good platform. Much better if I had some weapon—something to strike at the gun with. I scanned the roof. There were the two soft bags, empty, and the light, unmanageable water can. How right he'd been to throw everything into the moat! I needed something long and thin, and there wasn't anything. Unless . . . One of the slats, perhaps? Maybe I could break off one of the unattached ends.

I darted to my corner and heaved up a slat with all my strength. It bent like a bow—but it wouldn't snap. It was no good—they were coming back. I could hear them on the staircase. I forced the slat back and down until it was bent double and almost flat again—but it still wouldn't break.

Then, suddenly, I had a different idea. I held the slat down with my right hand and drew the blanket over the bend in it and sat down with my right elbow pressing hard on the free end. I'd just settled myself when Mollie's head appeared in the doorway.

Smith called out, "Where are you, Mr. Curtis? Answer!"

I was thankful, now, that I hadn't climbed on to the turret. I'd never have got away with it. I said, "Don't worry, Smith, I've given up. I'm over here by the wall."

Mollie stepped out. Smith stuck his head round the edge of the door, cautiously, and saw me. He grinned.

"So I hadn't a chance, eh?"

I said, "You're a murdering swine, Smith, but I have to hand it to you. That was quite a performance you gave."

"I thought it was pretty good myself," he said.

He made Mollie sit down, and he wired her up again. While he was occupied I shifted my position slightly and pulled the blanket a little higher. It looked all right from where I was. If only he'd hurry! My elbow was beginning to ache horribly.

He finished with Mollie at last, and resumed his seat beside me. "There they go," he said, as the rearguard of the cyclists disappeared over the hill. "Well, they'll never have a closer shave than that!"

I grunted. The pressure of the slat on my elbow was becoming unbearable. I felt the sweat break out on my forehead. I was afraid he might notice that one of the slats was missing to the right of him, but he didn't. It was the inside one that I'd grabbed, the one nearest the wall, and the gap was less obvious there. Anyway, his main interest was in the path and who else might come up it. The gun was in his lap. I didn't look directly at the gun any more. I'd be able to see any movement out of the corner of my eye. At the moment he was right out of range.

I was sweating all over now. I could feel the moisture running down my sides, trickling down my back. My face was dripping, but I didn't dare to wipe it. I didn't want to draw attention to it. I concentrated on keeping the slat down. I reckoned I could hold on for another couple of minutes, and that was all. I could feel the end of it biting into the flesh of my forearm. The fingers of my right hand were beginning to grow numb. Soon the whole arm would be numb. I moved a fraction of an inch, trying to ease the pressure, but the slat merely bit deeper. I tried not to think about it, about the pain. I began to count, slowly. One . . . two . . . three.

... Perhaps I could reach twenty. I *must* reach twenty.... There was still a chance, if I could hold on. I got up to fourteen.... It was no use, I should have to let go.

Then Smith moved. The hand with the gun came down over the slats beside him, not quite pointing at me, but very much at the ready. His favourite position. Sweat dripped into my eyes, so that I could scarcely see. But I could see enough. The barrel of the gun was over the corbel where the slat had been. So was his hand. I leaned forward slightly and jerked my elbow away.

Everything seemed to happen at once then. There was a rending of cloth, a loud smack as the slat hit the corbel, and a yell of agony from Smith. The gun went off and flew into the air. It landed on the concrete in front of Smith. I dived for it, just as he shot out a foot and kicked it out of my way. He scrambled after it—but he was too late. It went spinning across the roof towards Mollie. She picked it up neatly and threw it over the parapet into the moat.

I was at the door before Smith could reach it, blocking his way. For a tense moment we all looked at each other. Smith's face was like putty. Blood was oozing from the crushed fingers of his right hand. My own right arm was still numbed and useless. My coat was almost ripped from my back. I slipped it off and dropped it at my feet.

"Well, Mr. Smith," I said softly, "this looks like the last round, doesn't it? Let's see what you can do without your gun."

I knew he could do plenty if I gave him the chance. He still had a hand and two feet. The only time he'd be negligible would be when he was dead. I approached him slowly, watching him all the time. I feinted with my right—what there was of it!—and hit out hard with my left. The blow landed, but not heavily. He grunted, and put his head down, and came at me like a bull. He couldn't use his right, either, but with what he had he could lay me cold if I wasn't careful. I was careful. I sidestepped his rush, and hit him again. He was nothing like as agile as the first time we'd fought. His limp and his hand were against him. My right arm was coming back to life, now, and I used it. We weren't fighting for fun. I rocked him with a blow to the face and an uppercut to the chin and when I saw he was groggy I went in and battered him. I thought of how he'd slapped Mollie, and ripped her clothes, and kneaded me in the groin when he'd still had his gun, and I wasn't short of incentives. I went on hitting him, with all my strength. He didn't fall—he slowly sagged to his knees. I dragged him up and gave him one more for good measure—and that was the end of the fight. He slumped back against the wall, drooling saliva and blood.

My knuckles were flayed, but that was about all the damage I'd suffered. I rested for a moment while I got my breath back. Then I stepped across and slipped Mollie's foot out of the wire. "Nice bit of fielding!" I said.

She was very pale, but amazingly composed. "I'd better get the police," she said.

"Yes, as fast as you like. I'll be all right—I don't think he'll give any more trouble now."

She started towards the door—but before she could leave, Smith called out "Wait!" and she stopped. He struggled to his feet, and leaned against the parapet. He'd made quite a recovery, but I couldn't see him renewing the attack—and I was right. What was on his mind was something quite different.

He said, "Don't be hasty, Curtis—this is the chance of a lifetime for you. Surely you're not going to pass it up?"

I said, "What do you mean?"

He tapped his pocket. "These stones I've got here are worth fifty thousand pounds. You can have them—in return for the use of your car. You and Miss Bourne can share them. You'll be quite safe—they've been lost sight of for four years, they're not hot any more. No one will ever know. If you let me go, I swear I'll never tell anyone that you have them. If they catch me, I'll say I threw them in the moat. Fifty thousand pounds, Curtis! Think of it!"

I looked at him sadly. It was the only speech he'd made since our first meeting that wasn't in character. But then, of course, he'd never been in these straits before.

I said, "Carry on, Mollie. Let's get this over."

I stepped aside to let her pass. Smith's expression was desperate.

He pulled himself up on to his toes as though bracing himself for a last effort. I thought he was going to take another crack at me after all. But he didn't. He took a flying leap on to the parapet, stood there for a second, raised his arms above his head—and dived.

We both rushed to the edge. It was an incredible dive for a man in his state—a remarkable dive for anyone, fully clothed. He went vertically into the moat with hardly more splash than I'd have made from ten feet. He had such momentum that I expected him to come up near the bank. I was all set to rush for the car and intercept him. But he didn't come up near the bank. He didn't come up at all.

Chapter Twenty

That afternoon the police put a dinghy on the moat and recovered his body with a couple of grapnels. They had quite a job, because he'd gone head first into the gluey black mud and stuck there, and there was a lot of suction. His mouth, when they pulled him out, was full of mud. It couldn't have been a nice death.

Once they had the body, as well as our story, it didn't take them long to identify him. The Yard knew all about him. His real name, it turned out, was Walter Rance. Up till a few years back, he'd been notorious as a gifted cat burglar and jewel thief, with a flavour of Raffles about him. Lawson, who came racing down to Lodden that evening, goggling and almost speechless over our adventure, told us when articulate words finally came to him that he'd have known the man anywhere from the photographs he'd seen. But then Lawson specialised in crime, and had done for quite a while. As an active operator, Rance had been before Mollie's time, or mine, so we naturally hadn't recognised him. Not that it would have made the slightest difference to anything if we had.

The jewels, mostly diamonds and rubies, belonged to the Earl of Carisdown. They'd been stolen from his stately home on the South Coast four years earlier on the night of his daughter's twenty-first birthday party. Rance had been arrested in London about a month later, but on another charge. He'd been suspected of a hand in the Carisdown coup, but a woman had given him an alibi which the police had thought phony but couldn't break, and they hadn't been able to prove anything. He'd been jailed for four years on account of the job they knew about.

The Carisdown affair had never been cleared up. There had been a suspicious incident near Lodden the day after the raid, when a police car on special patrol had chased a car that had refused to stop. It had skidded and crashed on Lodden hill, overturning and bursting into flames. Two men had been trapped underneath it, and when the fire had died down their remains had defied identification. So had everything else in the car. The engine number had been scored out; the registration plates had turned out to be false. The two men were clearly crooks, but there had been nothing definite to connect them with the jewel robbery.

"When Hoad had been found murdered, and attention had turned to the missing key, no one had thought of associating the theft of the key with the car crash. If the police, on the day of the crash, had happened to notice a third man in the escaping car, the link might have been established—but they hadn't. Now it seemed more than likely that all these incidents were connected.

With Rance dead, the truth of what had occurred could only be a matter for conjecture, but the police reconstruction ran something like this. Rance had led the Carisdown raid, with two associates. For some reason that would never now be cleared up, the three men hadn't left the district immediately after the burglary but had spent the night there. Next day they'd set off for London. Rance had been in the back seat, and at the first glimpse of the police car he'd ducked down. When the car had crashed, Rance had been flung clear. According to the local records, a rear door had been wrenched right off in the smash, so that was certainly possible. He'd been carrying the jewels in his pocket. Knowing that the police were close behind him, and fearing an immediate hue-and-cry, he'd looked around for some safe place to hide the loot. He'd spotted the castle and crossed the fields and gone in through the open door while Figgis was hurrying to the scene of the crash. Up in the tower, he'd found a deep crevice in the ancient parapet and stuffed the wash-leather purse in. It had gone in further than he'd intended, dropping down out of his reach. On the way out he'd removed the door key, just in case he'd need more time for recovering the jewels than an authorised visit would give him. Presumably he'd intended to come back for them as soon as the heat was off, but the jail sentence had spoiled his plans. And that was about all there was to it.

It didn't seem a bad reconstruction. Certainly, no one ever produced a better one.

Chapter Twenty-one

It was an incredibly exciting evening—one of those occasions that
stay in the mind for ever. To be free again, with the shadow of the
gunman removed, with Mollie looking as fresh and lovely as though
her ordeal had never happened, with the office wires crackling
congratulations and even old Hatcher saying he'd like to buy me
a beer, with other and far more able reporters waiting for crumbs
from the rich man's table—all was wonderfully exhilarating. Not
that I had much time to bask at first, because the story had to be
written and phoned in time for the early editions, and there was
a lot of it to write. I was hard at it in my room for more than
two hours, and when I'd finally put the story over I needed a drink
badly. I thought Mollie might be in the bar, but she wasn't. I had
a couple of quick ones with Lawson, and then excused myself and
went in search of her. I asked the porter if he'd seen her and he
said she'd gone out for a stroll more than an hour ago. She'd
obviously got through her story much faster than I had. I still
envied her her skill and craftsmanship.

It seemed unlikely she'd have gone back to the castle after all
the unpleasant things that had happened there, but I walked up
through the fields, just to make sure. I spotted her almost at once,
down by the river, and quickly joined her. She was lying on the
bank, lazily twiddling a bit of grass in her fingers and gazing down
at the water. She seemed very relaxed. She gave me a warm smile
when she saw me, and patted the grass beside her invitingly. It was
the first time I'd seen her without a mob around her since we'd
gone for the police.

She said, "Did you get your piece off all right?"

I nodded.

"How are the hands?" She inspected my knuckles, and made a wry face. "It was quite a fight, wasn't it? You were most impressive. . . . In fact, Hugh, you were rather marvellous all through."

I gave a modest shrug. "You weren't exactly inactive yourself. Who grabbed him by the hair? Who tossed the gun away?"

"We were very lucky."

"We certainly were. What a story! How much did you send?"

"About half a column," she said.

I stared at her. "Half a column! You can't mean it. Why, I must have sent three columns."

"Fine!—it was worth it. I hope you really put yourself across this time."

"I certainly did, but . . . Mollie, what's the idea?"

"It's your story," she said. "You earned it ten times over. I decided to leave it to you." She smiled. "I wanted to say 'Thank you' in some way and that seemed a good way. The greatest sacrifice a woman like me could make."

"I'd be quite happy to settle for the second greatest," I said. "Couldn't you reconsider?"

For a moment she regarded me in amused silence. Then, slowly but emphatically, she shook her head.

www.ingramcontent.com/pod-product-compliance
Ingram Content Group UK Ltd.
Pitfield, Milton Keynes, MK11 3LW, UK
UKHW040105010325
455690UK00002B/20